Table of Contents

Prologue: Meet Joncy Ber..1

Start of the Plan's Execution...4

A Few Weeks before the Execution of the Plan.........11
    Exit Scenarios...13
    Outsourcing..14

Prepare for Future Retrieval of the Assets.................15
    Prepare Storage in Panama City...16
    Preparing Storage on the Cayman Islands...........................23
    Keeping Up Appearances...25
    Preparing Storage in Singapore...26

Gathering Valuable Information...................................28
    Assessing Target Clients..30
    Compromising Target Clients...32
        Password Reset from a Trusted Website for Wei..............32
        Phishing Mail Campaign for Jing..33
    Compromised Targets Wei and Jing......................................34

Hacking the Internal Network of China Bank...........36
    Crawler Bot..37
    Exploiting Vulnerability...39
    Remote Access Trojans (RAT)...40
    Retrieve Hardcoded User Credentials...............................41
    Human Resources Directory Server..................................42
    Active Directory Server...43
    Automate Steps to Obtain Credentials...............................45
    Transaction Database, Banking Software, Inter-Banking Network..47
    The Day after the Successful Breach....................................50

Cashing Out..52
  Prepare the Environment..54
  Active Masking of Running Operation..........................56
  Covering My Tracks..57

Hacking of States Bank's Internal Network..............59
  Phish Using Smaller Fish...60
  Exploiting Vulnerability...61
  Cashing Out...64
  Prepare for the Money..64
  Covering the Tracks...67

Collecting the Assets..68
  Flight to the Cayman Islands...70
  Cayman Islands Gold and Palladium Pickup.....................72
  Panama City Gold and Palladium Pickup..........................74
  Flight to Paris with a Bag of Gold....................................76

Cleanup of the Physical Devices................................79
  Flying to Hong Kong..80
  Dispose of All Physical Evidence....................................82
  Flying Back Home..84

A Year after the Hack..88
  Buying the Island..89
  Detection and Public Disclosure Dilemma........................90

Disclaimer..92

About the Author..93

Editors: Christopher Cervelloni and Michael Jauchen
Cover design: Genivaldo Neto
Map image design: Genivaldo Neto
Published by Press agency MOREL, Ljubljana, 2021
Printed on demand.
CIP was prepared by National and University Library Ljubljana
COBISS.SI-ID 64375299
ISBN 978-961-90983-3-2

I would like to dedicate this book to all my fellow tech enthusiasts who constantly face the security issues and gaps that have been introduced by fast-paced development and poor developer education. In this fight against illegal information gathering and privacy breaches, you are not alone. All of us can help contribute to our users' education so that the activities described in my story would be much harder to accomplish and would require someone to have much more knowledge.

Open-source software is a way of thinking and a way of life, so do not allow tools to be deleted just because they might make malicious activity possible. After all, closed-source software is abused even more and rarely gets fixed.

I want to thank my wife for the critical reviews of the initial drafts and for pushing me to make it more of a story. After all, I am used to writing technical documentation, not books.

Prologue: Meet Joncy Ber

Hi,

I am Joncy Ber, and I have seen Earth circle around the Sun about thirty times. We both know this is probably a lie, but you'll soon understand why I'm saying it. The following story is about my plan to get rich quick—actually, just to get rich quicker than the average person.

By all standards, I have had an average life. I live in a rented house, I occasionally eat out, and I play some sports. Even with all this, I've been able to save some money for the future. It's a habit I picked while working for start-ups, where you want to have at least two salaries on the side in case the company falls into rough times. I am not the world's smartest person, nor am I the best engineer, but I've worked in large, multinational companies whose products are probably sitting around you right now as you read this. If not the products themselves, then definitely the components inside them. I contribute to open-source software. For most of my career, I've earned a decent income. However, even with the best salary, in the tech sector, earning a million euros gross can take about a decade. And it takes even longer to net that much. I didn't want to wait that long, especially since I could not save enough to provide me with an early retirement and a carefree life in the near future. After all, even in the Western world, you are already considered old at thirty or so and you should start thinking about starting a family.

Anyway, you can decide for yourself if my story is real or not. Or maybe my story contains some truth, which is up to you to discover.

HONG KONG

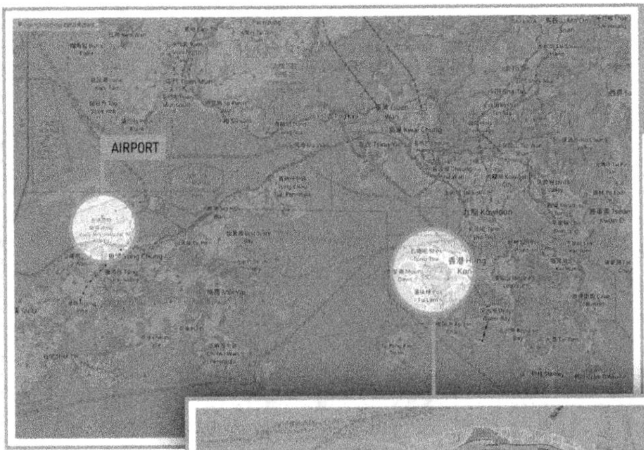

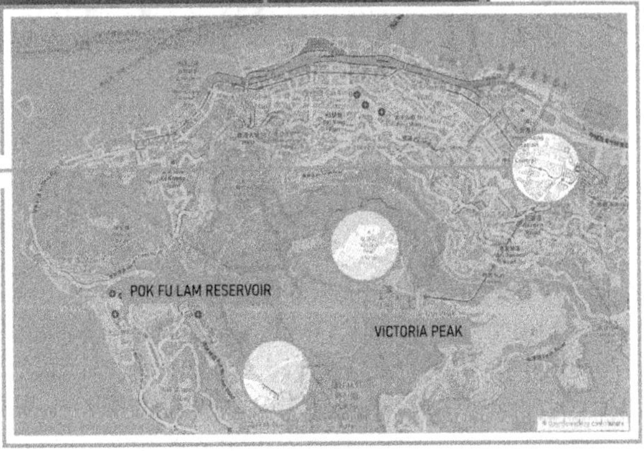

HONG KONG
CHATER GARDEN

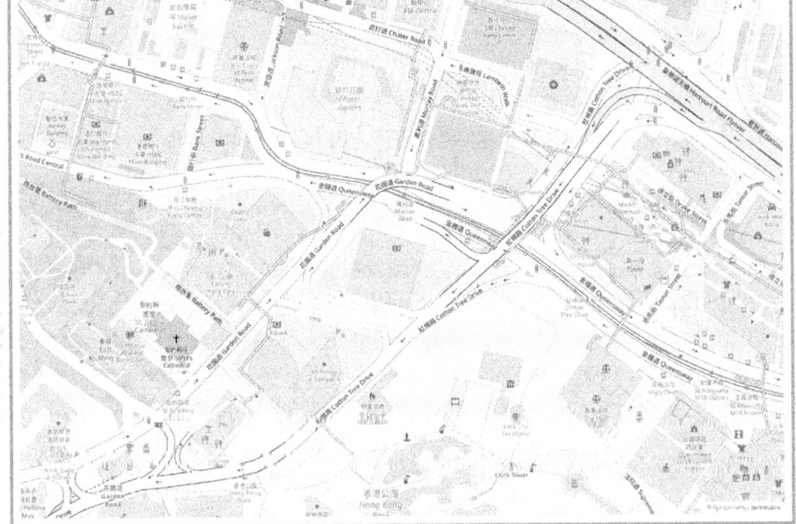

Start of the Plan's Execution

It was the beginning of summer, somewhere in the Benelux area of Europe, where the landscape is mostly grass with some small patches of green forest in between villages and cities. I lived in a small village and worked at a nearby multinational company. One early Saturday morning, I was ready to execute The Plan. To mask my true origin, a friend drove me through country roads to a bus stop in a bigger village nearby. The darkness was still hugging the landscape when the bus arrived, and as I boarded, the driver smiled at me. His fresh look seemed like he had just started his day. I walked past several passengers before reaching an open seat. I calmly sat there, only briefly scanning my surroundings every couple of minutes. I looked through my window as the countryside passed by and only glanced around a few times at what seemed to be regular passengers on their way to work and their daily routines. That morning, I had put on a fake mustache, and the day before I had colored my hair black. On the bus, I wondered if someone would think my appearance looked fake. As the bus drove through the countryside, more passengers got on. It was becoming a bit crowded, but at the first big town, all the passengers exited. The bus drove on for some time before reaching the airport, its final destination. As I exited, the driver said farewell with a faint nod.

I arrived at the airport just in time for my long-distance flight to Hong Kong. I traveled with my own passport. The disguise would help me claim that my identity had been stolen if the police later checked the video cameras that track everybody at all major transport hubs. Edward Snowden revealed that tracking persons with an increasing number of CCTV cameras is done regularly. I wanted to avoid the slight possibility that the forged identity I had obtained from shady characters on the dark web would get discovered by police. As I could claim my identity was stolen by a malicious actor, it would, at the same time, also provide me with some insight into the police investigation. Asking about my whereabouts would mean that they had uncovered all the other tricks I had used to hide my identity.

Inside the terminal, I went straight to the check-in kiosks to get my boarding pass. Even though I had a backpack with me, it made no sense to get a boarding pass from another location as that would make it simpler to uncover my real intent in any potential, upcoming law enforcement investigation. Then I walked through a nearly empty airport to the security check. I gave my boarding pass to a security agent who politely showed me the bins in which I should place my belongings. As usual, laptops and fluids need to be placed in separate containers. I opened my backpack and took out a bunch of small boxes holding RaspberryPi 4 computers. I placed them in a separate security box for the X-ray machine. Then I put my powerbanks in another security bin. The powerbanks ensured there would be enough power for a few weeks of operating the RaspberryPi's micro-computer that would be connected to them. In the third bin, I placed my backpack, which had USB splitters, a small LCD screen, and a keyboard.

Once, I left a Sphero Robotic ball in my bag, which, because of its round shape and electrical circuit, alerted security. I had to dig it out and show it to the agent. I thought they might just disassemble it at that time, but luckily, a transparent Spark+ model displays its internal structure. Because of that experience, I also knew that as long as you have valid answers prepared and can technically explain what various devices are used for, the devices can then be taken on the airplane.

The check went through without a glitch. Nobody asked anything. Nobody noticed the 3D-printed watertight cases that ensured weather would not affect the RaspberryPis' insides, and nobody questioned me about my multiple powerbanks. At that time, there still wasn't a ban on batteries in hand luggage on flights. Otherwise, I would have had to place them in my checked luggage.

It was a short walk from the security check to police passport control. My mustache was the only thing different from the black and white photo on my national passport. I was assuming that it was not going to be suspicious at all, yet I still picked the personal check instead of the computerized one. It also seemed logical for maintaining the minimal digital footprint I wanted to leave. I started to queue for the police officer. I watched the people around me as I waited a couple of minutes for my turn. I casually walked to the box and handed the officer my passport and boarding pass. He glanced over the photo and my name on the passport and then just waved me through.

I had passed one of the risk points in the whole plan. I was expecting it to go smoothly, but I at least expected some remark about my new look. I continued to walk through the duty-free zone, past the shops and toward my designated gate. As I glanced at the clock, it showed that I was ahead of schedule. The smooth security check and passport control meant I still had forty minutes before I had to board. I decided to spend that time in a toilet near the gate. As boarding started, I took a few additional minutes before I went from the toilet to the gate. I entered the queue of other passengers who were waiting to board. I was wary of my stance and the location of the security cameras. I was trying to avoid directly looking into them, which might later serve as incriminating evidence of my presence. I only waited in line for a couple of minutes. The stewardess smiled at the gate as I approached her and gave her my passport, putting my boarding pass on the barcode reader at the same time. She took a long look at me as she wished me a pleasant flight. As I went past her to the airplane, I found myself again in the more or less private space of the aircraft. I put my backpack in the overhead compartment and then took a seat.

I filled the fifteen hours on the plane by watching movies and sleeping, just to ensure I was well prepared for a quick run around Hong Kong. Later that same day, I had a return flight to ensure I would be back at my day job before anyone noticed. As I left the plane and walked through the corridor into the Hong Kong Airport, I entered a big terminal, which was a humbling experience. From the gates to the airport exit, I had to take the train, and then I walked past all the duty-free shops, where I resisted the urge to spend some money on cheap tech toys. As I walked past the arrival hall, I took a taxi to Chater Garden, which was right in front of the various banking towers and other major bank headquarters in the vicinity. I had scouted the park with Google Street View many times, but I focused on the distances between various landmarks as I walked over it for the first time. I was constantly looking at my phone that had a passive wireless sniffing application that was surveying the surrounding Wi-Fi networks. I had no problem blending in with the business crowd in the park, as everyone was focused more on their phones than on the nice park around them. The park had many places to hide my RaspberryPi devices. I noticed the plant pots near the park entrance, and I thought for a second that they would be a great spot to put a device. But as I walked a bit further, there was too much risk; the plant pots were quite high and might expose the device. Not far away, I walked past a thick green curtain of climber plants. They would perfectly camouflage my devices and shield them from direct weather. I had a few more tasks to complete before finally planting my devices at their final destination, however.

Walking down the Queensway, I was able to get into the local telecommunications shop where I bought pay-per-use SIM cards for GPRS modems. After that, I walked into a local restaurant for lunch. I loved Chinese cuisine and ordered some noodles. I had time to think, and I decided to place the GPRS hubs behind the climber plants in the park. I already planned to put the RaspberryPi devices in the plant pots closer to each of the buildings on the park's edges, but the GPRS hubs would be much safer if they were hidden in the thick leaves. The distance between the pots and the climber plants was small enough for the Wi-Fi to cover, and they seemed like perfect hiding places, even for a long time. The noodles were delicious, and with a full stomach, I went to the nearby shopping mall where I picked up the worker's uniform that I had ordered online. To avoid suspicion, I went to the toilet there, where I got dressed. On the toilet, I also installed the local SIM cards into the GRPS modems and connected them to the RaspberryPis that acted as a hub and exposed the whole network of other Wi-Fi sniffing RaspberryPi devices to the internet. Nobody noticed the change I went through, so in the end, I walked toward Chater Garden and Lambeth Walk Rest Garden, posing as a public worker checking the plants. I walked from the sidewalk, past a small strip of grass toward the big tree right next to the overpass. I used my hands and a small screwdriver to dig a small shallow hole near the roots of the tree. I placed the first RaspberryPi device in the hole and covered it with dirt. I noticed the people walking over the overpass. Then I glanced at my mobile phone and saw that there were many wireless networks in the vicinity. Next, I walked a bit further toward some elegantly trimmed bushes that lined the low hill. I dug a shallow hole among them and placed another RaspberryPi device in it. Once I covered it with dirt, the device was well hidden. I knew from the Google Street View photos that the palm trees in the center of the park were a bad hiding place. They were bare at the bottom, and they only had a small patch of soil exposed around them before the curb and walking surfaces started. However, there were some Agave plants at one side of the park, which provided a lot better cover. I put the two devices among the Agave plants on each exit at that side of the park, so that even if maintenance watered the plants, they wouldn't be able to spot them.

The device mesh was placed and powered. I used my mobile phone and a commercial Virtual Private Network (VPN) to connect through the Tor network and get the initial analytics from the whole system. That would ensure everything was set up correctly before I went back home for some long hours of browsing through the data to find the useful information. The small LCD display and keyboard I had brought with me would come in handy in case one of the devices was unresponsive, but to my surprise, everything worked flawlessly. Just like I had tested at home. That meant I had time to kill. I decided to visit Victoria Peak to avoid the temptation of beginning to hack right on the spot. I knew there was no local camera network in the green forest of the Victoria Peak. Before all this, though, I had to dispose of my workers' clothes. I used a parking garage toilet to swap my clothes and stuff them into a trash bag, which I carried to the dumpsters behind the back entrance. I had checked the available photos online and knew that there were dumpsters there.

The sky was sunny and cloudless, and I started ascending a twisty route toward Victoria Peak. The scenic walk provided me with views of the Hong Kong skyscrapers below that towered over the city. Once I reach the top of Victoria Peak, the whole island became visible, and the bay glittered from the sun's rays. The hike was not that long. After that look over the city, I descended the other side of the park near the Pok Fu Lam Reservoir. It is an artificial lake in the middle of the hill, and on the lower side of it, there are already some apartment buildings. I walked to the main road and took a taxi back to the airport. Since airports have the most cameras and watching eyes, I needed to spend as little time as possible there. I did not want to give away any personal traits that could later connect me to my actions, so while walking through the airport, I made sure that I did not scratch my nose or bite my nails. The security check was routine, but the passport control officer did run me through a computer before waving goodbye. The flight was on time, and the boarding started just a few minutes after I arrived at the gate. Boarding on the big Airbus A320 also took a while, but once I was in my seat, I tried to relax a bit more. As I landed in Brussels, I took the bus in a different direction than the one I'd used on my first trip. After a few bus stops, I got off and joined my friend in a car. We drove home through the country roads. Once I got there, I confirmed that my home computer was continuously executing a couple of activity scripts from a USB flash drive. The next day, which was Monday evening in Hong Kong, the whole network went online and transmitted the processed data through the Tor network toward my home Kubernetes cluster. The Kubernetes cluster analyzed and visualized the data for me so that I could decide what to do with it. I still needed to be in the office for my day job, which would provide me with a great alibi.

A Few Weeks before the Execution of the Plan

There is a lot of preparation if you want to successfully infiltrate a network without detection, especially if you cannot dedicate your full time to it. This was my pet project, but to be honest, my professional focus isn't computer science, and I do not know much about hacking. I know how Wi-Fi is built and how to use Aircrack or Wireshark to debug network communication but making an automatic data parsing tool that will only send back valid data, along with a Command and Control server, is something beyond my skill set. Luckily, I learn fast and can spend a lot of evenings and weekends producing the perfect set of tools for the job. Then came the obfuscation of the code, removing the debug information and comments, and, of course, a lot of testing. The idea was that the multiple RaspberryPis would gather information by sniffing Wi-Fi networks in the near vicinity, but then during the night, they would process data as the Kubernetes cluster while only sending useful information like Wi-Fi keys, emails, decoded email contents, and passwords through the RaspberryPis with a GPRS gateway using the Tor network to cloud server. That way, I could access the data from my home. The device mesh ensured that even if one RaspberryPi was compromised, the others would be harder to discover. Nightly processing of the obtained information ensured that there would be no big data stream back to the cloud server, and to make it better, I set it up so that it had to be triggered by a predetermined handshake. I also securely designed the case so that if someone tempered with it, the RaspberryPi General Purpose Input/Output pins (GPIO) would detect it and send an alert back to the master before starting to write random data over the SD card and then slowly destroying the RAM content. The network would also be aware of the rogue MAC address (Media Access Control address is a unique identifier used as a network address in communications within a network) and consider the hostname and keys as invalid. More so, it would then be tracking this new MAC to follow the investigators' progress.

As the project developed, power management also became an issue, and I decided to let the node devices go to sleep during the dead hours but still report back afterward. I took this from various existing networks where, during the night, the device could request a next scheduled check-in after a couple of hours. That does not mean the master goes to sleep, but it does mean the device is not bothered with the commands from the master devices during that time. However, the master nodes had bigger powerbanks connected to them and were the main contact point. To avoid excessive battery usage, the master devices did not do much of the processing, but just handled communication and coordination. I had managed to seamlessly connect various tools into one decent, deployable surveillance network. The primary purpose was to disguise my location and alert me in case of outside detection. You would think all the items I've listed above cost a lot of money, but the investment was not even 1,000 euros. That included all the 3D-printed special casings and water/dust protection that were required for longer runs.

Exit Scenarios

You always plan for the worst but hope for the best. Even with simple product development, it is better to finish before the deadline than to be late and disappoint everyone. So The Plan had various exit scenarios at different stages of its execution and always provided an optimal way to destroy the existing evidence. As someone once wrote, it is not about what you know but about what you can prove.

The initial exit scenario was that during testing, local police would be alerted of the suspicious activity around my house. Since I doubted that they would actually have a warrant or that they would execute a raid, the simple excuse here was that I was learning about Kubernetes. Somehow I doubted they would see a simple case from the outside and wonder about everything going on inside it. The next exit scenario meant that all development had to be done on USB flash drivers. Code was developed with the git version control system, but it was stored only on the USB flash drive. Commit authors were anonymous, and there was a fake John Doe user. I doubted that they would ever find them, but I still hid them around the house during the development and plan execution. After the deployment of the nodes in Hong Kong, the exit scenarios diverged as did the included risk factors. I was not about to cancel the whole operation just because some worker discovered a working device in the bushes. I was also not about to start panicking if the entire network was exposed, but I had written and stored and analyzed every idea of what could go wrong for weeks before I executed the first step.

Outsourcing

If you are doing everything yourself, you risk going over the deadline. That is why getting multiple people to work on the same project is such an important thing. However, considering hacking and its mostly illegal background, the fewer people who know, the less risk there is. I will bluntly claim here that I did everything myself, but that is just a lie. Actually, I just don't want to implicate the other people who were actually unintentionally helping me with various tasks at hand. There are many platforms, like Freelancer, where you can get people to do simple tasks, but the tasks need to be general enough so that they cannot be connected to hacking. You should never write, "Please obtain a password from my girlfriend's Facebook account." But if you state this differently—saying something like "I would like to decrypt my old password using a list of passwords"—you will get many tools and tutorials on how to do it. Again, the person-hours invested in the plan were massive, but the end costs were not even a single salary due to the cheap outsourcing of labor.

Prepare for Future Retrieval of the Assets

The first weekend deploying the devices, I drove toward the airport in the early morning. The evening before, I had dyed my hair and eyebrows light brown to adjust my appearance. I had also let my beard grow for the whole week and dyed it light brown. I took country roads to the opposite side of the country as before, just to sit on the bus alone the whole way to the airport. As the bus was driving through the pastures and villages, my mind floated around all the steps I had to take this weekend to ensure that when I actually obtained the money, I could liquidate it without much risk. This step from the virtual to the physical was usually the riskiest.

Prepare Storage in Panama City

This time my hand luggage only included a toothbrush, laptop, a small tube of toothpaste, and a few clothes. I really wanted to avoid waiting for checked baggage and all the messy pickups, and I didn't want to run the risk of losing my luggage just to have to report all the different destinations where I would be. The check-in machine again printed my boarding pass with an aisle seat. I blazed through security, but some businesswoman in high heels stopped my eye. As I passed through the police checkpoint, I again used my real passport. That morning, I had looked in my mirror, and I didn't exactly look like the person on the passport photo, which to my surprise, also drew some attention from the police officer at the passport control box, who took a bit longer to look at my passport and me. He smiled and told me I look much more manly than in my passport photo. He asked me about my birth date and nationality, and I answered him politely as I smiled and thanked him for the compliment. Once again, I walked through the duty-free area toward the gate. I needed a much shorter toilet visit this time around, but as I arrived at the gate, the intercom announced that boarding was delayed for an unknown reason. It would be suspicious to go back to the toilet, so I found a place on the opposite side of the gate on the seats looking at the takeoff strip and parking tarmac. As I was chilling, a woman approached me to have a chat. I recognized her as the same businesswoman who had drawn my attention at the security check, and her questions seemed to be causal traveler's chat. She was actually going to Miami International Airport as well, but for me, that was not the final destination. Women had never approached me in the past, especially not in random public places. So my mind went ballistic with scenarios involving undercover agents and police, which might uncover my plans.

Her looks, though, did not reveal anything suspicious. Her makeup was mild, and her nails were polished and shorter, which allowed her to type on keyboards. Her jewelry was quite expensive, filled with crystals, and she wore matching earrings and necklaces. I answered her standard questions honestly, and she told me that she worked for a big corporation in the sales department and that she was a frequent traveler. Now my thoughts went to a scenario that she was straight from the bank security team and that they had uncovered my system and phishing scheme. They could also send people undercover to see how many people were involved on my side. But soon our conversation turned to our casual hobbies, lifestyle, and even sports. The sports part confused me, but her figure showed she was quite active. Time flew by, and the flight had already started boarding. I glanced at her name on the boarding pass and memorized it. Let's call her Mrs. Sunshine. As she searched for her phone in her purse, I saw a key ring from a basketball team, which I took as a sign of her interest in sports. We talked while boarding, and I noticed that I also got more attention from the stewardess at the gate. Not just a simple smile and "have a nice flight," but more of a smile and "please tell me if you need something." It was a strange situation, especially with all the things going on over the past few weeks. As we boarded the plane, I thought about what I had planned my answers to be in case I got questioned. I had a transfer flight from the USA, so I would not actually be going through customs. I would not be entering American territory, which meant they couldn't arrest me there. I knew one of the banks I was targeting originated from the USA, so if they had uncovered the mesh network, then they would want to arrest me in the States. It was also a bit too early for the warrant since I had hardly done any damage, although US law, in this case, is not much different. On the way to my seat, I kept the conversation going, just to see where she was sitting. As I got to my seat, I noticed she was also starting to prepare to sit down. She had a window seat almost next to mine. Some time passed, and it seemed like nobody was going to take the seat between us. Once boarding ended, it became apparent that the middle seat would be empty. Again, a strange coincidence? As the plane taxied away from the terminal, we both started to focus more on movies. Or maybe that was my reaction to our ever-shorter list of general conversation topics. As takeoff began, she seemed a bit pale. It was a strange reaction for someone who flew a lot, so I made a remark about it and she bluntly replied that she hated the acceleration feeling right at takeoff. To me, this reply did not match the sporty appearance from our previous conversations, but I did not push the topic and quickly focused back on my movie.

After takeoff, I watched the movie and, on the side, did some Google investigating into my fellow traveler. All of the things she said seemed genuine. Mrs. Alice Sunshine was a Sales Department Chief at a company selling routers and wireless access points, which also had offices in Europe. It was a strange connection to a field that might be affected by my plan's actions. What was more surprising is that her LinkedIn account showed that she had graduated from MIT in computer science. How could an MIT graduate end up in sales? As I found that out, the stewardess came by for the first meal. I wanted to avoid meal conversation with Alice, so I was reluctant to put my headphones down, but because it would be really impolite, I decided to pause my movie. While we were served, our conversation went back to general work-related topics, and Alice mentioned that she was, in fact, interested in computers and network security. I steered the conversation topic toward that fact, mentioning that I was developing devices that relied on network security. This was then our topic for the next few hours. We had a vivid discussion about various solutions and implementations. We shared a common view of open-source software's importance in keeping security tight because a public auditing was always possible. We got chocolates for dessert, and I casually mentioned that I had a sweet tooth for milk chocolates. The stewardess heard my remark and afterward got me a few more, claiming that a few other passengers had not taken them. I took it in stride and kept the conversation with Alice going. A few hours into the flight, she said she wanted to take a nap, and I really needed to stretch my legs. I walked to the plane's common area and stood there a bit when the stewardess, Pam, started a conversation—not a casual "it's a nice flight conversation," but about what did for a living, how much I traveled, and where I was going. We chatted a bit, and I found out that Pam had worked as a stewardess for only a year after taking a break from her physics studies. She was interested in signal and energy transfers, so she had studied that for her PhD. Again, some of the technical chat about the topic made the time fly by, and as lunch was about to be served, Pam had to do some work. We chatted while she was preparing everything, and the other flight attendants did not mind at all. I went back to my seat so that she could serve the meals to passengers, and I knew Alice did not want to be disturbed by the meal. Alice already told me that in case she fell asleep, she did not want to be woken up unless we had landed and were taxiing to the gate. I suspected she took some sleeping pills before the first meal when I was watching the movies. As Alice was peacefully sleeping in the seat next to the window, Pam served me a meal, and I completed the movie I was watching. It was time to take a toilet break and stretch my legs again before I planned to take a nap as well. Daytime naps were hard for me, especially while sitting, so I was not looking forward to it. As I was stretching my legs, Pam was again in a chatty mood, so time flew by really fast. I had to excuse myself to get back to my seat, and I took a nap. I was asleep in minutes, and it seemed like quite soon, Alice was rubbing against me. She was awake and wanted to go to the toilet, so I just smiled and moved aside. As I wanted the aisle seat, this was not a big problem at all, but I thought she would sleep longer. I glanced at my watch, and I had been asleep for three hours. When Alice came back, Pam was already serving our last in-flight meal. We were about to land in a couple of hours. Alice was in a chatty mood once again, so we continued talking about the technical topics from before. Time passed so quickly and we were soon getting ready to land. We kept up our lively conversation, and Alice did not seem to be as bothered by landing as she was at takeoff. I also kind of forgot that after landing, I could actually be arrested or questioned. As the plane came to a halt, that reality kicked back in. I had a connecting flight in four hours, and the gate was in another terminal. When I left the plane, I said goodbye to Pam while Alice was walking right behind me.

In the terminal, I looked around and there was no police presence visible. I knew that airports are literally covered with cameras and that they could track me easily. As I kept the conversation with Alice going, we came to the crossroad where she had to head through customs and I had to go through a one-way transfer door. Alice asked me for my private email address, and I gave her the Proton mail account I had prepared for such cases. After a short farewell, we separated. It felt strange. Had I just been questioned by an undercover agent? Had they already uncovered my mesh network and were they trying to see if I had the knowledge to operate it alone? As I was walking to my gate, my mind had time to process all the events over the past few hours. Was it my updated appearance that had attracted all this attention? I was tired, so I decided to find a seat in the airport lounge, set the alarm on my prepaid mobile phone, and take another nap. After a refreshing sleep, I could again think clearly. As I arrived at the gate, the boarding was already well underway, and I was again greeted pleasantly by the counter staff. As I boarded, the young flight attendant also greeted me with a bit more affection. On the packed flight to Panama City, I sat next to a few businesspeople who kept to themselves. We were still served in-flight meals, and the young flight attendant served me. I completed one movie and then decided to stretch my legs again at the back of the plane. The young flight attendant, Elise, was there, and she started a casual conversation. She kept the chat going, and when I told her I would be in Panama City for just a day to do some business, she told me that she had a degree in business management. We didn't have much common ground until I discovered she was a huge book fan. Elise loved thrillers and also wrote a blog about her adventures in cities she visited between flights. This was enough content to keep our conversation focused on blogging, online revenue, ads, and our adventures around the globe. Time passed by quickly, and we were soon about to land.

As Elise came by for the final check, she asked for my mobile number. I couldn't refuse, and it was a prepaid phone, so I just gave it to her. She entered her email address and told me to contact her if I felt bored in Panama City. I don't know if she noticed the lack of contacts on my phone, but looking back, that was something that I could have improved for situations like this.

Once we landed at the Tocumen Airport, I felt that I was not being watched as much. I went through customs without any glitches and was soon on my way to find suitable addresses for my shipments. It was Saturday there, so I had already made appointments for outside normal working hours for a substantial fee. You can open a company online, but then some documentation is sent to your residential address, and to avoid this, I basically went to Panama City in person. As I drove toward the bank, I worried about the process of opening a few bank accounts. But the super attentive clerk who greeted me did not even bother to cross-reference all the details, like the fact that I was opening accounts for a few companies. After all that was done and the applications for the companies were filed, I had some time to kill, but I was not yet bored. In Panama, you have a few addresses where you can receive shipments. They then resend those shipments to addresses you specify or store them until you come to pick them up in person. Of course, there are costs for both those services, but that was not something I was worried about. I had made all the arrangements in person so that when the physical assets arrived, I could store them and then reship them to where I needed them on demand. I was relying on anonymity for security, so I was severely underestimating the value of the packages that were to be received.

By late afternoon, I had finished all my tasks. My flight to the next destination wasn't until early the next morning, so I felt a bit bored. I contacted Elise and she quickly responded back with the address of a restaurant on Flamenco Island. I gave the address to a taxi driver and continued to chat with Elise, who was apparently already at the restaurant. She had just completed a visit to the Nature Center and had posted some beautiful photos on her Instagram account. Luckily, I was not overdressed for the occasion, so I wasn't embarrassed. The food was excellent, and after dinner, we went for a walk to the top of the hill on Flamenco Island before concluding our evening in a hotel. We both had early flights to catch, so it was great not having to slip out of the room without breakfast. As I was leaving, she told me that she had been assigned to a smaller airplane going to the Cayman Islands. I did not tell her that George Town Airport in the Cayman Islands was also my next destination.

Preparing Storage on the Cayman Islands

We shared a taxi from her hotel in Panama City to Tocumen Airport, where we parted ways. Elise never asked me where I was going, which was great as I could act like a regular passenger again. Although Tocumen Airport seemed to have less surveillance, I did not want to leave anything to chance. I still walked directly to the gate and tried to avoid any cameras. Before boarding, I casually went through the boarding gate to the airplane. It was a small Boeing 737-200, and as I got on, Elise gave me a casual greeting until she recognized me. She seemed genuinely surprised, which was a relief. The flight was relatively short, and the weather was nice. During the flight, I again went to stretch my legs and talked to Elise for basically the whole time. She was fun to be around and knew a lot about managing a business. As we landed at George Town Airport, she had to work on the plane's next flight, but I had some more tasks to do. We were able to say a much more intimate goodbye on the plane this time.

Because of that, I ran across the terminal toward customs. I queued for some time, but I was still distracted with my thoughts when I answered the customs officer's questions about my reason for the visit. In the end, they were happy enough to let me into the town. It was Sunday, and I had special meetings arranged to complete all the legal stuff on the Cayman Islands as well. While I was there, I also reserved some addresses for receiving shipments and opened some companies to cover my tracks. The first meeting was in a storage building almost next to the airport, and the following meetings were in the vicinity as well. The Cayman Islands are not big, but I did not see a beach or sea that day. After a few hours, I returned to the airport, went through the simple security check, and walked right toward the gate where boarding for the flight to London was almost complete. It was a bigger plane this time, and as all my tasks for the trip were successfully completed, I could relax a bit. On this flight, I also seemed to attract some friendly looks from the female flight attendants. I sat next to two uninterested younger people, so I watched a movie before the first meal. After all that, it was time to shut down the lights as most people would go to sleep. That was the best way to eliminate the upcoming jet lag, so I also tried to sleep. It took some time, but I fell asleep for about seven hours. Then I went to stretch my legs by walking around the back of the plane. The flight attendant got up some courage and started asking me causal questions about the flight. She did not develop the conversation any further, as Elise or Alice had, so I returned to my seat and watched movies for the remainder of the flight. After landing at Heathrow Airport, I was again exposed to much higher risk. The number of cameras and focus there is really high, but there was no way I could pick another airport, as this was the only way to arrive back in time to get to my day job. I had to take a risk and hopefully blend into the crowd. I also knew I should not try to avoid cameras too much, as it might attract unwanted attention. Luckily the transfer time between flights was short, and I did not even have to wait for boarding to start, as I was already on the plane back to Brussels. It is a short flight where you barely have any time, and once I was back at the Brussels Airport, I again took a bus to a nearby village where I was picked up by car and driven home.

Keeping Up Appearances

After I arrived home, I shaved my beard and colored my hair back to its natural color. Then I had to go to the office for my day job until the end of the workweek. The jet lag started just two days after I arrived back, and I decided to sleep it out as I had done before. The following weekend, I had another set of flights to the other side of the world. Good planning helped here because there was basically nothing much I could do besides my day job. I had used quite a few resources on my flights to Hong Kong, Panama, and the Cayman Islands, but my plan involved one more flying weekend. I did not want to have my resources geographically tied to one another, and I wanted to have them spread out as much as possible to avoid suspicion when that many assets would be located in one location. As Friday approached, I finished my job early. I still needed to change the color of my hair again, and some beard had grown back, so I needed to color it as well. Luckily, I have fast-growing facial hair, and this was helpful to maintain the natural look of my disguise. I also did not have much time, so I performed these tasks while the driver took me toward Amsterdam airport for an evening flight to Singapore. I chose to fly from the Netherlands that weekend, mostly because of the direct flight connection, but also to avoid showing Brussels airport as a focus point.

Preparing Storage in Singapore

Because of my tight schedule, I could not take a bus to Amsterdam airport. I exited the car in a village two bus stops away from the airport. That way, I made it a bit more difficult to be tracked in case they were already on my tail. A long line wound through the security check at Amsterdam Airport due to the evening flight. I did not lose much time at the check-in machine, and I was also traveling light. When it was my turn to go through security, I completed it quickly, and I was already on my way toward the police checkpoint for international flights. My flight had already started boarding by that time, and I was running a bit late. My foxy orange hair and beard this time around looked more similar to my black and white passport photo, so I was not delayed. I ran through the terminal toward my gate and just barely caught the boarding. The flight attendant was already preparing for the flight, so I rushed to my seat. I was sitting next to a young couple. Soon after takeoff, it was time for another airplane meal. I must say that even though I was eating a lot of them, each meal was something special and tasted great. There had the feeling of eating in a decent restaurant, although the food was in plastic containers. Long-distance flights always have something magical about them, and the couple next to me was a tad bit strange, but they were occupied with each other and did not mind me. I had ample time to rest, watch movies, stretch my legs, and just enjoy the experience. It was a pleasant flight, but we landed in Singapore in a storm. That meant the descent was a bit bumpy, and because of the side wind, there was a last second realignment before the landing. It is quite exciting when you know how it is done and you are watching it from the passenger window. After we safely arrived, I went through the terminal to the city exit. The police checkpoint was not a problem again, and I was soon looking for a taxi outside. The taxi took me the short route to the storage location near the airport. I met with an employee there and explained to him that there would be a few shipments coming in by the end of the month and that he should just store them in my storage room. He was OK with that and told me that this was how they operated and that privacy was their utmost value. That was great to hear, and I rented the box with the credentials of my Panama City company. After the storage space was rented, I had a plan to create a proxy location, which would only forward the shipments and not store them. Singapore also offers that type of service, and I had a set up a meeting to do that on Saturday afternoon. As I arrived to arrange it all, I reserved the proxy under my personal name so that it could be part of the stolen identity story. I paid in cash for the half-year just in case the hack took a long time. As I was walking around Singapore for some sightseeing before catching an evening flight back to Amsterdam, and as I took a taxi back to the airport, I did not notice anyone following me. The security check was swift, and I was picked randomly for the explosives check. Nothing else was worth mentioning, and I was already at the gate when boarding started, so I just got on the airplane. Watching the other passengers board reassured me that I was not being followed and that my activity had not yet been detected. A young man sat beside me on this flight, but we did not talk at all. He watched movies the whole time, and I read. When I went to stretch my legs, a chatty young passenger began talking to me just outside the toilet. He was flying home after visiting his family and was studying in Amsterdam. He explained to me some major cultural differences between Europe and Singapore, and the discussion was quite interesting, but I soon excused myself to finish reading my book. As we landed back at Amsterdam Schiphol Airport, I was satisfied that my task was completed so easily. The police check for entering the country was again not a problem for my foxy orange disguise and soon I boarded the bus away from the Amsterdam Airport toward Haag, where I exited at the second stop to switch to a car, which drove me home.

Gathering Valuable Information

Once the network was deployed, a number of people dropped their Wi-Fi connections to nearby Wi-Fi networks, and as they reconnected with WPA (Wi-Fi Protected Access (802.11)) handshakes, the passkeys were slowly revealed. In fact, in just a few days, I could unlock all the Wi-Fi SSIDs (Service Set IDentifiers, or basically the name of the Wi-Fi network) in the area, discovering most of the hidden SSIDs and their keys in the process. All these tasks were executed automatically, and slowly, usernames and passwords from local users got extracted from the pile of gathered information. It is amazing how careless people are in public, and also, the local GPRS (General Packet Radio Service—basically, the cellular communication network) repeater caught useful mobile data information. But for that, I knew they would be on quite fast, so it was turned on just during identified rush hours and later on, only during the stage when the target client was passing by the area. After I received usernames and passwords, I used the remote network VPN server to obtain more information from the plain web. That way, I could identify CEOs (Chief Executive Officers), IT (Information Technology) department chiefs, and other softer yet still valuable targets like Marketing or Sales Directors. The gathering of the information never stopped, but the real news was that once you hit the limit of the gathered data, the growth stops, as most people have a daily routine.

Because of all the extracted information, an active attack was not needed. An active attack means that devices forcefully disconnect someone from a network or close their connection so that they have to reconnect to an existing network. And with that reconnection, the protocol's key handshakes are performed, which with existing unpatched security holes, enables the extraction of the true Wi-Fi network passkeys. People tend to think of connectivity as something constant, and they never consciously notice that their mobile phone is disconnected from Wi-Fi, just to reconnect back to the same network a couple minutes later. With the emerging high speed broadband mobile networks, most of the time, devices automatically switch between Wi-Fi and mobile connection, resulting in many more protocol handshakes.

In the past, robbing a bank required a gun and a gateway car. Today, you only need a keyboard with a computer and brains to cover your tracks. Bank security has also evolved, and while the gun scenario is still considered by banks' security teams, hackers have done the most damage in recent years. The amounts of money stolen and hidden in cyberspace are much higher and require a different kind of protection. Improvements toward the gun scenario means that collateral damage is not in civilians' and bystanders' deaths but in privacy breaches. This was just omitted in my plan as it did not draw enough value in effort versus time.

Assessing Target Clients

I do not care if there is some Lee cheating on his wife or if there is a Leilah stealing money from the cashier. There is not enough money I can gain from either of those clients in typical scenarios to cover the effort of obtaining the information and the time I needed to extract the money. I am not saying that I deleted such gathered information, but I did not use it during this part of the plan simply because it was not worth it. If Lee is a millionaire or has a wealthy wife, who he does not want to divorce, then that could net a couple of million. On the other hand, it could also increase my exposure to law enforcement, which could uncover the underlying infrastructure and jeopardize the whole plan. The same goes for Leilah. Unless I could somehow persuade her to steal more frequently and then take my share from that, the amount she had at her disposal would be nothing compared to my end goal.

My real targets, as mentioned before, were the more influential people inside the banks in the vicinity of the park. People in those organizations would have enough access to sign or confirm higher value transactions. There are many ways to find out who your targets are. Public directories list various people working at different companies. You need to link those names from public directories to existing usernames and emails you obtain when gathering information. After you make that link, you can start compromising the whole organization. In case those employee directories are made public, then this connection can be easily created, and more personalized emails can be written. But nowadays, organizations like to hide their internal hierarchy, and this was the case with companies around the area I was looking at. I used the first credentials I could get and tried them to access the banks' internal network through the exposed intranet page that the target client had accessed while walking through the park. An employee was maybe checking some things or just reading the internal newsletter, which uncovered the URL of the internal website. I could then use the same path to access it again with the target user's credentials. This disclosed all the information that I needed to identify the higher value targets at the bank. Because banks have various security protocols to ensure people do not access the network outside of their normal working hours, I needed to consider all of these things when performing a long-term attack. I identified Wei, the finance department head at China Bank, and compromised his social network account. From States Bank, I identified Jing, a disappointed lower-level employee who was reading the recruiting agency's website as he walked through the park, and stole his email address and other information.

Compromising Target Clients

After assessing the valuable target clients, I needed to decide my vectors of attack. There are always many options, and some might be better suited to certain people than others. Also, dedicated targeted phishing emails can be crafted when you know internal structures and procedures. Any information gathered and obtained in previous stages should be used, and it is even better if you can obtain copies of the emails or maybe even order procedures. Remember, with all this information I gathered, I was still on the outside of the system. I needed to compromise the computer on the internal network to gain direct access. At this moment, I already had several valuable clients, and I decided to pursue two of them, who would later bring the biggest return of value back.

Password Reset from a Trusted Website for Wei

I obtained Wei's username and password for his social network account, which provided a great option for copying the website reset password mechanism to deploy the malicious payload to his work computer. I risked that he would open it from his mobile device but mitigated the risk by schedule sending my email at the moment he was in the office, behind his stationary computer. The time stamps of when he walked through the park indicated when he came to work and when he left. It sometimes also indicated that he took lunch or business meetings outside of the bank, which left me with only a few small windows when I could perform the attack. I also risked that Wei would trigger the reset process while he was at a meeting, which would lead to a compromised mobile phone instead of a computer. I considered all of this as I prepared a password reset email for his account. I added the information I obtained in the email to make it personal enough so that it would be plausible. And then I sent it.

Phishing Mail Campaign for Jing

I composed another phishing email mimicking LinkedIn InMail. First, I found a recruiter on the target's friend list. Then I pretended to be a recruiter by sending a stolen look of InMail, asking him to check the job specifics for a new opportunity that paid a lot more than what he currently earned. In the email, I attached a Microsoft Word Document file with macros, which then triggered the download of the malicious payload and a trojan horse. After I sent the email, all I could do was anxiously wait for a bite.

Compromised Targets Wei and Jing

When a phishing campaign starts, this is the first time you are entering an illegal sphere. Up until that moment, you have not done much that is unlawful, but phishing schemes are illegal. Usually, with targeted phishing, you receive almost instant feedback if there is a successful bite. Wei literally took a bite in minutes after I sent the email. That is the moment that trojan software got installed, but I did not want any additional activity on the network. Such activity would trigger the alerts in the target organization. To avoid detection inside the China Bank network, I waited a couple of days before proceeding. Jing also opened the email using his office computer, which established an initial foothold inside States Bank.

Each organization has its own infrastructure and architecture of the whole IT system. It also has a different organizational chart and different security restrictions, which are in place to make the banking software and inter-banking network as safe as possible as a whole. But there are always flaws that can be exploited, which is where hackers come in. You can be a white-hat hacker, which means you disclose your information to the target company, and you first ask for an agreement that you can hack the organization. But as a black-hat hacker, you are in it for your own benefit. You get paid by the money you steal or by the information you sell. I had had a bad experience as a white-hat hacker once, when only proper paperwork saved me from some people covering their ass. I was amazed at how protective they acted when I just showed them areas for improvement, but as a black-hat hacker, you do not have to worry about that. As a black-hat hacker, some people have tendencies to do damage to the internal networks and organization, but in my opinion, those are just thugs. They are similar to thugs that riot on the street and crash shops while protesting against the government.

Hacking the Internal Network of China Bank

After a successful phishing campaign on Wei, I waited an additional week to ensure that more activity on the target computers did not raise any suspicions with the traffic monitoring tools, which were sure to be deployed in any decent organization. As I was still working my regular day job, I started hacking only in the afternoons and at night. So on a rainy day, after I came home and took a shower, I started the operation of mapping the internal network of both organizations. At this point, I had to prioritize my time, yet I had to divide it so that there would not be too much traffic in either organization. In this chapter, I will describe the hacking of an organization where I obtained access through Wei, who was the head of the finance department. Because of the time difference, the evening in Europe is actually nighttime in Hong Kong, and Hong Kong, which is in a regulated bank environment where certain work schedule restrictions are applied. So money transactions in that timeframe are out of bounds but looking around the infrastructure is a bit less suspicious. I prepared a stack of chocolates that would fuel me throughout the night. Initially, I drew a map of the hostnames by obtaining and querying the local Domain Name Server (DNS) for the domain list and at the same time tried to identify some other human-readable descriptions of the possible targets. Once I got the important server names with their IP addresses, I deployed a crawler bot to do the job. While the bot gathered information, I could start checking the results. Port 80 is commonly used for the web server and querying the web server on port 80 usually gets you at least some sort of webpage. They are usually not password protected since they should only be available through the intranet, but they can contain a lot of private information. Some of it was interesting, but unless it was some IT department list containing usernames and passwords, they were not that valuable to me for the time being. I noted down all the details on my local wiki, took another piece of chocolate, and continued the exploration of the downloaded list. The first entry on the list was from a recently updated server, so I discarded it as a potential target as it would actually be a more challenging target to attack.

Crawler Bot

I had a script that gathered and sent the data to the internal computer I had compromised. These scripts are usually called robots or crawling robots or crawler bots as they work broadly in the same way a Google search engine robot does, except that they have a lot more features than just mapping a website structure and extracting the keywords. My bot used Nmap (an open-source program) to scan the open ports. As expected, most had ports 80 and 22 open. The main goal was to figure out the name and version of the web server and other programs that were listening to the open ports. Once I obtained that, I could then compare the known vulnerabilities and just use them to gain access.

One of the things such a robot needs to be careful of is not to create too much noise. For example, suddenly asking the whole network of servers on their open ports for the programs and versions will create a big chunk of traffic. A large amount of traffic on an internal network should be detectable by any decent IT department. And even if they weren't, it would create a massive slowdown of the local network, which would be bound to manifest problems elsewhere. It is then up to the security team and the IT team to identify the source of the slowdown. So the bot needs to spread the load. It also needs to be a bit more random. Imagine a user who requests a new site every ten seconds exactly, down to the millisecond. You might guess such a user does not exist. So there are tools on the local network which detect such periodic activity and send an alert about it. While such tools might not be installed on the target local network, it is easy to add a random delay in the crawler bot query script to avoid such incidents.

As the crawler bot was providing me data, I forwarded it to an external network. Also, here are a couple of detection mechanisms you need to be aware of. The first is that the TCP/IP (Transmission Control Protocol) socket to external IP (Internet Protocol) is opened for a significant amount of time. The exact value for this significant amount of time is again something you establish on a case-by-case basis. Still, an example here is that someone is uploading a lot of internal information to the external service. This is considered a huge security leak and is also something network monitoring tools are aware of. The second example is opening many connections to the external device, which could indicate the transfer of a lot of files. This is also something monitoring tools are detecting. Trying to defeat such tools usually means you only log in to issue commands. Even better, you only leave commands that are then taken by the compromised internal computer as confirmations of the received data. Of course, you are actively logged in at the start, so you need to be careful to avoid detection. In this case, I also had one of my scripts watching my fingers. I called it a "guardian angel" script; it would alert me at random time intervals to logout from the ssh session. Otherwise, everything was pretty much automated at this point, and the data sent to the external network relayed through the compromised servers all around the globe.

That way, data was not sent to the single external service, was not sent by multiple connections to the single external service, and was not even sent in big chunks. It just mimicked the standard browsing pattern of querying multiple servers every couple of minutes.

As I was going through the received data, I also used my local computer's script to check the vulnerability database for known vulnerabilities. This was something I was doing most intensively that night, and of course, it was just a matter of time until I found a vulnerable server. In the case of the China Bank, one of the webservers had a vulnerable PHP-fpm5 program running. That meant privilege escalation could be forced, and I could gain root access over the server. That was the weakness I was looking for, and one that actually would justify actively logging into the compromised internal server to exploit the vulnerability. I needed a second compromised computer in the network to mitigate the above issues of a single crawler bot, and that you can't really automate. Each server is a bit different, and each has a different configuration and settings. Before I accessed the server, I took another piece of chocolate, stretched my fingers, and started the "guardian angel" script.

Exploiting Vulnerability

As a hacker, this is the moment you live for. Time is running out, and while you can have a lot of automated protection, there is also a slight chance that the security team has already detected your bot and is trying to pinpoint your location. Data has to come somehow to and from the hacker, so the security team has various ways of determining the hacker's location by the actual router location. They can pinpoint that to an apartment, and if they get access to your internal router or Wi-Fi, even an area inside an apartment. So actively exploiting the vulnerability is a fight against the machine and other smart, maybe even smarter, people.

I never got nervous in such cases, although the penalty, if I were to get caught, was severe. Because I had a decent crawling bot, I already knew the first line of defense and some other side remarks, so I could prepare an attack plan before the time even started running. As I logged in and executed the script to defeat the vulnerability, it was only a matter of seconds before I knew about my next obstacle. In this case, there were none, so I got root access to the server. I uploaded a Remote Access Trojan (RAT) and another crawler bot to help spread the load. As this deployment was done in the background, I was also searching for possible ssh usernames and passwords, along with the command history of any strangely mistyped commands. Once that deployment was completed, my job was literally done for the moment, and I started covering my tracks. That meant deleting the executed command history and login times as well as clearing any logs for errors, which might be logged as I exploited the vulnerability. Once that was done, I would log out from the server and go through the obtained data locally.

Remote Access Trojans (RAT)

Remote Access Trojans are used to gain access to a network using multiple points. They would be helpful in case my initial position was compromised. I suspended those RATs, which meant that they would contact the RaspberryPi network in the park every couple of days, just to try to figure out if they were needed. I also used their servers to send data obtained by the crawlers to avoid detection by automated network traffic tracking tools. In my case, the whole attack masqueraded as if it was originating from the park just outside the target organizations.

Retrieve Hardcoded User Credentials

As I was going through the recently obtained data locally, without the time pressure, I discovered that PHP files contained hardcoded usernames and passwords to some other servers. I extracted and saved that access information as it meant that I now had an actual user or maybe even admin credentials to access another server in the network. I provided the IP address of that server to my crawler bot as a priority scouting request, which meant I would get all the information about that server in the next scheduled try. That included an ssh login with those credentials to the server. As I anxiously waited for the results, I took a short walk around the house. I could not hear any rain outside, and darkness hid the hedge around my house. I left my lights off as I went to the fridge to get some juice. It was a major success that I had most likely obtained valid user credentials to another target in the first session, but I still had to be alert. Too much activity, or even the wrong activity, with those credentials could trigger some alerts. In my mind, various scenarios were unrolling.

Once, when I was on vacation, I wanted to gain access to the hotel Wi-Fi. I managed to sniff the SSID key and then I used it. After thirty minutes, I was permanently redirected to the page, which told me that I was not authorized to use the Wi-Fi network with that SSID. It was persistent as it was bound to my laptop's MAC address. Some security teams ran a really tight house, and I certainly wasn't going to underestimate the bank's own security team.

I sipped my juice slowly and thought of another scenario where hacked credentials had gotten me nowhere. It had been in an organization where the access credentials were created like tokens. They had a username and a token as a password, but those were only able to access certain IP, and what was even worse, they could only access it within a certain timeframe. That meant that outside of the requested timeframe, the user credentials were denied, as if they were invalid, while in the requested timeframe, they worked with the intended limited access on that IP only.

Back then, the first part drove me mad for few days until I directly mimicked the script's behavior. After that, I found out that user credentials only gave me limited access to that particular server. That dead end wasted precious time. And since those credentials were added to the list of valid credentials, it also meant one try when brute forcing credentials got wasted with each newly discovered server in the whole process.

Human Resources Directory Server

I put my glass into the dishwasher and started to walk toward my computer. Which of the cases was I going to uncover this time? I had had some previous experience, but the thrill of the whole thing is that it is never the same. While the enemy is different each time, there are some general tricks that are usually deployed to deter the least experienced hackers. That is why there are various online services where you can try different methods. They also test your fast thinking in terms of how to breach the server. My computer screen illuminated the room, and as I unlocked it, the hunt for compromising the third server began. Meanwhile, the bot had already sent me the report. The credentials worked. The server seemed to be some sort of user directory server with internal employment information. It was a gold mine for employees' private data. I wanted to investigate more, so I logged on to the RaspberryPi mesh in the park and from there, through the initial computer into the China Bank internal network. I used the credentials to ssh to the employment server and looked through the pieces available to me. This was by no means without risk. If I tried to access information that this user usually didn't access or wasn't allowed to access, it could trigger an alert. The first thing I tried to retrieve was the personal information of the user whose credentials I had obtained. I found that the user was actually one of the IT team members who specialized in an internal project for employment statistics. That meant that he probably used his own credentials to extract employment information for further processing. I had the script, so I looked over it quickly to see what all would be available. With such a beginner's approach, I expected that there would be unlimited access. The script was accessing all the employee information daily and presenting them. I looked forward through the directory carefully, gathering IT team names, roles, and projects they had worked on to formulate the opponent's strength. Those credentials allowed me to view everything from birth dates to marital status to salaries and bonuses. I scraped as high as I could go, and before leaving, I also looked at the personal information of the head of finance, whose computer I had initially hacked. Sometimes such minor things can come in handy, especially if you face those pesky security questions when trying to perform something unusual.

Active Directory Server

I looked at the other open ports my crawler had discovered and noticed that the server was also listening on port 389, which was the default unsecured Lightweight Directory Access Protocol (LDAP) port. This meant that the LDAP database was updated with credentials from the employee server, so I decided to intercept the incoming packets on that port. An unsecured port meant I could read plain text activity on the port and identify a fourth server in the network, which was the Active Directory server. A secured LDAP port 636 would make it a lot harder for me to decipher it all. The Active Directory server is mostly used to store user access credentials, authenticate users, and also set permission rights for the users. It is a key keeper for most of the gates in a company. Usually, such servers have extremely tight security, but from time to time, the network architecture, like in this case, leaves some vulnerabilities. I looked more closely at my current server and noticed that there were some similar roles, which might have been the base for the access. I created the employee with the role of a higher IT member with basically the same name as the existing real employee, except that I used look-alike Cyrillic letters as replacements for the Latin characters. This meant that it was a new employee for the computer, but for someone looking through the graphical user interface, it would display precisely the same way as a real employee. What was even cooler was that it would not appear in a search, as most searches are triggered on the first three letters, so if the second letter is a Cyrillic replacement, you will never get that person. It is a simple trick you learn as a non-English native where character sets matter. I set the loop on the email port of the server and waited. I did not want to log out again, and I hoped that the refresh would come soon. After a few minutes, it did, and with the second piece of chocolate in my mouth, I intercepted the email to the new employee with the login credentials. I tested the new credentials immediately as I tried to ssh into the Active Directory server from the Human Resources server. It worked. The permission level was automatically set to be very open, based on the role I copied, and it meant that most likely, these would open many doors. In such cases, you always want to limit the amount of time these credentials are in the system, as it might occur that the finance department would try to pay your salary each month or simply that someone would notice a strange user and report it back to IT. But I had a way to generate these credentials on the fly. Now all I needed to investigate was what would happen when I tried to delete them.

The night was still young, however, and the sun wasn't yet rising over the misty forest behind my house, so I could use the newly obtained administrator credentials to explore the network even more deeply. I entered the new credentials into my crawler bot to check if I could log in to a couple of other servers it had identified previously. I set a time limit of three hours, which was just one hour shy of sunrise, which would give me just enough time to also clean up the credentials from both the Human Resources and Active Directory server. I cleaned my tracks on both servers and decided to take another break as I let the crawler bot do the exploration. When cleaning my tracks, I searched for all the access logs and deleted entries from the terminal history. It was a quick clean, but I did it just in case someone went looking into those logs. I knew I still needed to come back and remove the new user from both directories.

Automate Steps to Obtain Credentials

While I was waiting for the crawler to do its job, I wrote a simple script to create a user, intercept the email, and store the credentials to the crawler bot on both servers. Completely tuned to this organization's IT architecture, I also wrote the draft of the script for removing the user. I always do the manual actions first, before letting a script do its job, just in case something different comes up. I remembered a past experience when I wrote a perfect script that would intercept the email to the user I was working with, but I forgot to intercept another email to the superior of that user, informing him of the cleanup action. The script missed it, but my eyes looking at the logs did not, so I had to then access the internal mail server and delete the mail while also deleting the access logs and all the other tracks I had left behind. It was a messy job, and a one-minute deletion operation ended up involving three hours of constant concentration and the hacking of another server. Lesson learned, and I did not want to repeat that mistake again tonight with a much more challenging target. If the script worked as intended, it would give me on-demand access to anything in the network while nicely clearing my tracks before somebody might notice. The premise was that nobody was accessing employee information overnight. Automation also helps so that you do not forget certain steps in case you are in a hurry. If I was detected, I could just run a script from RAM, which is hard to trace as there is no evidence on hard drives that it ever existed. It also saves time and allows an automated crawler bot to operate with credentials when necessary. Of course, I could only do this during certain timeframes, like deep in the night, but the crawler was smart enough to perform such high-risk operations only then and mostly on the limited number of servers I had selected.

After the script was written, the crawler still hadn't completed its tasks, so I had time to stretch my legs again. The chocolate slowly vanished as my brain wasted the sugar, and fat was starting to thrive. I needed some fresh air, so I walked out to the terrace just to get some fresh air. I was deep into illegal activity by then. I had already breached a substantial part of the network, and I had also accessed some valuable information. There was some money to be made selling the private employee information on the dark web, as it included all the necessary information for producing a perfect identity for identity theft. I quickly glanced over the dark web market and noticed that the identities of high-ranking employees at a respectable bank could be sold for a few thousand US dollars. That kind of identity theft can do a lot of damage and can even fake business contracts with less skilled companies. I looked outside my window. The mist had already started thickening among the trees, and as I looked at the moist air, my breath started to feel a bit heavy. Or maybe it was the task at hand. Walking back to my computer, I decided that both the Human Resources and Active Directory servers were not decent targets for RAT deployment. They were probably better maintained and might detect the running RAT. So I needed to find another target, and I also needed to identify the server for the money transactions. At my computer, I quickly glanced at a crawler report. I discovered that with the provided credentials, all the servers were accessible. That meant that the permissions were high enough to gain root access to the whole infrastructure. I knew that money transactions probably required someone from the finance department to access and would only operate at certain working hours. But IT can usually at least monitor those transactions, and the crawler report narrowed it down to two possible targets.

Transaction Database, Banking Software, Inter-Banking Network

Money transactions and account balances are usually something that you find in database servers. Because of high security, the data is of course encrypted, so it is not like I could just open an account and change the balance to a few million. There are also various security checks that prevent balance sum mismatches, so you need to learn the system so you can mimic real transactions. Luckily, I came in through the computer of the head of the finance department, which meant that the computer contained a lot of information about high-value transactions. They were also nicely time-stamped, and for some reason, the transaction database did not encode the time stamp. Maybe it was for simplicity's sake or it was just bad software development, but I precisely pinpointed the row in the database that had all the required information. One of the columns seemed like the seed, so with most of the data at my disposal, I used the computing cloud to decode the key. Anyone who's a little tech-savvy would call out my lie here because I didn't mention that the other server identified by the crawler report contained the banking software, which had the keys stored as environment variables. I extracted them using the popular Meltdown bug. Information is always fragmented for maximum speed optimization and, of course, for security. But the software that displays all the details still needs the keys, and decryption algorithms are usually written in the manual or the software configuration. Because I had direct access to the server, I easily extracted them. With all the pieces in my possession, I would be able to perform real transactions, but I still wanted to make them invisible and undetectable. What good does a virtual number on an account do if they arrest you once you try to withdraw the money? Usually, high-value transactions alert someone or even require approval from someone. While banking software is usually core to input and display data, there are other tools that monitor the integrity of the database and update the external balances with other banks or financial organizations. I targeted the external balances. I wanted to get money out of the bank without triggering the alert on the bank I was hacking. If other banks found out about the problem, it would take some time before they figured everything out, and my plan depended heavily on that. So to do that, I had to convince the tools that monitored integrity that the database's integrity had not been breached. At the same time, I had to issue external transactions to various outside accounts, which would allow me to buy real-world assets before other banks in between could figure out that the money had no origin. The plan's idea here was simple. Banks talk to each other the whole day, and at the end of the day, they cross-reference the balances. This is something called the SWIFT network. So while transactions through the day are ensured by each bank separately, the end of day balance is a check that basically amounts to the money the banks own between themselves. Since all this is quite hidden, it was never intended that someone would actually have access to this vast network. It was also not accessible from the organization's internal network. Still, through some other tools, the transaction server did have access to that network, as it needed to report the balances and transactions. Banks are also very in thrall of logging. Every transaction has a verbose description of the actions, and in my case, this helped me understand what actions those big transactions from the head of finance had triggered. Again, the process that was designed for protection became a source of information, and as I dug through the logs of other transactions, I found that they had the same trigger. I also uncovered all the access logs and drew UML diagrams of all the actions. Not only did I manage to breach the transaction database, but I also managed to decode all the transactions and uncover the network's whole system and safety mechanisms and how they worked. I reached my target for the night, so I had to cover my tracks on the transaction database server, the banking software server, and some monitoring tools servers. After that, I still had some time left before sunrise to install more RATs on the network. I knew the risk of detection increased with each RAT, but so close to the prize, I could not afford to lose access at that point.

The crawler detected a few other low usage servers that could provide a nice home to my RATs, so I simply logged into them and installed the same script on the first server that I had breached. Sometimes these forgotten servers are the best way to hide. Still, at other times, you manage to hit some development server where the developer monitors the processes and discovers a foreign process on the list. If that happens, you basically manage to uncover yourself. I also cleaned my tracks on those servers easily and then started to delete the newly created identity in the Active Directory and Human Resource servers. As I logged on to those servers using the initial credentials, to avoid triggering any alarms when the deleted user logged out of some active services, I started the deletion process. As expected, there were a few other mails and logs sent out of the Active Directory server when a user was deleted, and I managed to intercept them all. Then I also deleted all the logs in the Active Directory and Human Resource servers before performing a routine cleanup of the terminal history. This would make a forensics investigation more difficult, if not impossible, later on. As the last action of the day, along with a few more pieces of chocolate, I completed the automated deletion script to perform exactly the same tasks I had just performed. This also helped me retrace my steps, and mentally, I am always trying to find something that I missed or that I should do differently. I had probably completed all the actions well before the first employee entered the bank that morning. My in-park mesh reported virtually no activity on the Wi-Fi networks in the vicinity. It also meant I had time to go back and clean some more in case I identified some issues. Also, no activity meant most likely none of the IT guys were rushed to the office to mitigate the ongoing attack.

The Day after the Successful Breach

I breached the China Bank that night and anxiously waited in fear of being discovered. I was searching through all the obtained data and notes to see if I had missed something and to adjust the plans and prepare the scripts. The sun was already starting to rise on the horizon, the yellow and orange sparkles illuminating the moist air outside my house, when I decided I needed some sleep. I knew my day job should continue on as normal, even though the feeling of being a millionaire in the near future had started floating around my mind. Imagine it—I had the ability to perform untraceable million-dollar transactions almost on demand.

I woke up a bit late the following day. After I ate my breakfast, I cycled to work. That actually helped me reset my mind and get some fresh air into my lungs to clear my thoughts and completely wake me up. After a shower at the office, I was refreshed and focused on my tasks. But the day passed by slowly; like dead slow. I knew something, but I could not brag about it to my colleagues, and to be honest, it was not even related to my day job. I was never in contact with high-end application security or even IT infrastructure development or maintenance. It was so far removed from my day job that most coworkers outside of my team actually put hardcoded credentials into the plain text files. Luckily, I had a full agenda of tasks and no meetings, so there was no time to think about the mistakes I might have made the previous night. At lunch, I had some interesting debates with colleagues, which made the afternoon pass a bit more quickly. After work, I sped home. When I arrived, I immediately went to bed to be well rested for the coming morning. I fell asleep sooner than I expected, as I was pretty tired from the night before. As the alarm clock woke me up a bit after midnight, I had started to plot

the attack to steal as much money from the bank and transfer it to
less traceable digital currencies and commodities.

Cashing Out

When I woke up after midnight, I decided to go for a run to clear my head. I still had a couple of hours before the bank's business hours would allow me to make money transactions, and the plan I had prepared in advance was well developed. Now I just needed to polish some rough edges. As I started running, my thoughts cleared and focused on the task at hand, which was moving my legs and breathing. It was a dry night with a slight wind blowing from the West. That meant no mist and no clouds, so a sky full of stars. After I came to the end of the neighborhood, I turned toward the nearby forest paths. I was running without headphones and with some dimmed lights. My mind's focus shifted from moving my legs and breathing to the task I was about to perform. Taking money from anyone is a serious offense. While banks do have a bit more of an official approach, using the police to arrest you rather than killing you, the stress of performing illegal activity still provides a huge adrenaline rush. I did not know if I had somehow been detected, if they were already preparing to lay a trap to trace me, or if they had simply cleaned out my RATs to prevent further tampering.

This was something I prepared for by developing the exit strategies, but before you actually login to the server, you are in total darkness. The security team usually works regular working hours, and if I had tripped some alarms somewhere, they would have had time to investigate and prepare. Usually, hackers do not persistently infiltrate their targets, and that is for a simple reason: the less time you are logged in, the lower the chances are that you will get caught. But my plan was solid, and I needed an alibi, which I had by going to work each day, acting normal. I knew they could always argue that I could have done it during my free time in the evening, but I had also made an effort to increase my traffic each night in the nights before the attack, and for months previously, so that there would be no visible peaks during the time of the hacks. And most of the data was automatically assessed by the crawler bot and then exchanged with the RaspberryPi mesh in the park. That meant I was just accessing the summary reports most of the time, except when I was actively breaching the security. This all managed to provide me with a plausible alibi in case law enforcement ever suspected me.

As my running route entered the residential area again, I had a clear and fresh mind. The run was short by my usual standards and the pace was easy, although looking back at the data, the pace was faster than usual. As I arrived home, I showered and cooled down, and then prepared a quick meal. Chocolate corn flakes with rice drink was a great way to stay hydrated, get content into my stomach, and get the energy to start my day. After that, I drank some more orange juice and prepared the chocolate bars for the evening to come. As my computer got the recent updates from the crawler bot and mesh network, I looked through the data to spot any additional discrepancies that my automated scripts might have missed. It is mostly just a human habit not to trust automation in a new environment, but the stakes were so high that I have also fallen to the temptation. I put the plan and execution charts on a separate screen. I looked at that screen and highlighted my current task, which helped me focus. I had perfected this system with minor training hacks in the past, and I was confident that it would help me perform even on this bigger scale. The previous night, I had accessed the system in the middle of the night, without many people watching, but this time, it would be completely different. I would be in the system during the working hours when everyone was on the network, so the chances of someone stumbling across the fake user were a lot higher. Also, in case someone opened a transaction list and noticed strange transactions before they were masked, it could also raise suspicion. And opening an incident ticket for IT to investigate would mean that they were right there and ready to investigate. Now my enemy was not just automated systems, but also people But because of banking process restrictions, I had no other option.

As I had everything prepared, I opened a chocolate bar and took the first piece. I always resort to sugar and chocolate to fuel my brain and ease the adrenaline in such high-stress times. Outside, it was still dark and quiet, but in Hong Kong, the day was in full swing. The RaspberryPi network displayed the usual morning activity in the park, and my head of finance had already passed the park and was probably in his office. When I logged in using the RAT again at around 4:00 a.m. my local time, there was no sign that I had been detected on the previous day. The logs were the same, and there were no additional logins. I knew based on Wei's agenda that he had a full day of meetings. I first isolated his banking computer so that it cached packets and delayed them for few hours. It was all green and nice, so the idea was to use an internal inter-banking network to hide my transactions and to avoid stealing from people or, by accident, some more dangerous organization like the mafia or a drug cartel. Every inter-bank transaction gets verified less rigorously when it is between banks and when the amounts are high enough. That means stealing 100 million US dollars is a lot easier than stealing 10,000 US dollars. With that in mind, I was aiming to secure around 400 million US dollars in a matter of minutes, but that was still just an odd number inside the bank's account balance. As it was with every heist, the problem wasn't getting to the money, but in getting the money out.

Prepare the Environment

I ran the script to create one employee with an administrator IT role in the system and another one with the head of finance role. The two users allowed me to access and modify the whole system while also having the correct bank's internal process permissions to approve and sign large transactions. This went off without a problem, and I received both credentials. I logged in with administrator credentials to the transaction server to capture and delete all the logs as the new head of finance performed various high amount transactions. First, I created a virtual bank account on the China Bank with a deposit of 100 million US dollars. As soon as I made a deposit, the second user, the new head of finance, approved it. Now that the money was created, the transactions from this account could occur. But 100 million US dollars is not what I was targeting, so I created six more accounts with more random high amounts. It all went smoothly, but I did not want to leave these accounts open for too long. I used these accounts to purchase various things from sellers who did not have accounts at this bank. That way, the transactions would be lost in the inter-banking network and could only be discovered in the final bank transaction balance. I also knew very active accounts could be flagged, but I took that chance. I deployed a script that listened to any alerts to minimize the risk. After that, I executed the script that made transactions for purchases on various cryptocurrency exchanges worldwide for Bitcoins, Litecoins, and Monero cryptocurrencies. The biggest share of the purchases was for Monero, as it provides the best anonymity. But the purchases did not stop there. Imagine you need to spend 400 million US dollars. You soon start running out of ideas, especially since most cryptocurrency exchanges only hold certain operational amounts, so you need to be careful not to trigger alerts on those accounts. That is why I also had accounts on various asset-buying websites where I could purchase gold and palladium and have them shipped to various addresses worldwide. There was one huge setback I forgot to consider, however, and that is that the demand for certain assets increases the price of them. The market reacted a bit, and that spike is still visible on all historical graphs today. The irony was that right after my purchase, the price increased, but it also meant other people started buying as the uptrend continued. So once my purchasing was done, the price kept increasing. It meant that at the end of the day, as the assets kept their value, I had gotten richer not by 400 million, but by 650 million. Nobody knew at the time, and most likely, even today, nobody can explain the unexpected spike in digital currencies as well as gold and palladium, which match to the day.

Active Masking of Running Operation

During the operation, I was actively intercepting and then masking, removing, and approving alerts within the banking software. With the administrator credentials, I made sure that the logs were constantly cleared of the suspicious operations and also that the other daily bank operations were not affected and ran smoothly. I ensured the integrity of the transaction database by preparing the environment, but still, the transactions were one of the things that might be spotted by the people looking at the database. I put the access security of my transactions to the highest level, which meant only a small number of people would have the ability to even spot them. I also deployed another listening script that constantly monitored most of the compromised tools and intercepted any traffic related to my transactions. As all the transactions were completed and approved by the inter-bank network, confirmations of my purchases started to pour in. My focus remained on the active operation I was performing, although every confirmation distracted me slightly. If the scripts missed something, I needed to react as quickly as possible.

Because nothing much happened during the execution of the scripts, it was possible that I would become tired and lose focus. But in the past, I had already had that experience. In a previous, unrelated hack, I compromised a small company's network. It all ran smoothly. So in the middle of the operation of retrieving the file system content, I went to the kitchen and got some juice from the fridge. I also craved some chocolate, as it was a hot summer day and the sun was shining directly on my desk. I let the scripts execute unsupervised for just a few minutes. When I came back, the connection to the hacked network was terminated. As I wanted to inspect the files I had obtained, especially the last few, to figure out where it had paused, there were some usual looking docx filenames. However, when I opened them, they downloaded crypto locker software and locked my computer completely. It was a custom fixed crypto locker from the company I had just hacked and a message explaining the situation and asking me to transfer some amount of Bitcoins to the Bitcoin address. It claimed that I would receive an unlock key, but all the data obtained in that folder was already deleted before the encryption. I transferred the money and considered it as a fee for my inexperience. Still, after a careful investigation of the logs, I noticed, that, in fact, a file on the target filesystem had been created during my automated script execution, and my automated script had automatically downloaded it as it refreshed the index after each couple of downloads. Precisely after the target file was downloaded, the connection was forcefully terminated from the server side, which was not apparent from the logs. Still, it was something I would not have missed while looking at the terminal output flow.

Covering My Tracks

In the middle of the workday in Hong Kong, I basically took money from the bank and had it outside of the bank network, but I still did not have it in my possession. When all the transactions were complete, I deleted and cleaned all of the compromised accounts, deleted all the deployed RATs and crawler bots, deleted all the terminal command history I had touched, and cleaned all of the files on the compromised computer of the head of finance, Wei. In order to maintain the integrity of the transaction database, I couldn't delete the transactions themselves or the virtual accounts associated with them, although the balance on them was zero. Because of the Cyrillic characters, I hoped that it would confuse people looking at the transactions as something the head of finance had approved, but that he would deny for sure when he was confronted about them. It should take quite some time to figure out the trick and even more time to figure out where that account had come from. It still meant that once mistakes were uncovered, they might cancel the transactions, and this was the greatest risk. If, at the end of the day, they uncovered the fake transactions and managed to flag them, then I would not get anything except for cryptocurrencies, which would most probably be tracked as well.

As I removed all trace of my presence, I completed the whole hacking part of the operation. I sat behind my computer for a while, watching the movement of the Bitcoins from currency exchanges to the various wallets I had prepared. As I tried to make as many transactions as possible between those wallets using the digital currencies, they all ended up in just a few wallets. I mainly focused on transferring the funds to Monero cryptocurrency, as that is the most anonymous currency currently trading with a high enough, real-money value. After this, the digital part of the operation was completed. It was still a regular workday morning, and I followed my daily routine. As I drove to my office, knowing that this was probably a historic feat, doubts still existed in my mind if I would be able to get most of the physical assets that were ordered with the unbacked transactions in my possession.

Hacking of States Bank's Internal Network

I breached States Bank through Jing, and after the initial login, I deployed a crawler bot. I sniffed some ethernet packets to figure out the DNS and gateways and map the infrastructure to identify the list of servers that could be targeted by the crawler. After that, the crawler was left to do its job while I focused on other tasks at hand. Another night, another thinking process—yet the goal was the same. As the crawler was probing the resources on the network, I looked through the employee's hard drive. I found some transactions for lower amounts and a few documents electronically signed by his superior. That got me the name of the superior and some of his colleagues, but also the names of a few cashiers who were probably the recipients of the documents he had created. I did not find any direct access software for the money transactions on his PC, but the documents indicated that he issued orders for transactions. I dug deeper into his browser history to figure out that he had actually accessed the webpage, which was not on the local DNS. It was accessible through the internet and was a lot more secure. The mapping of the network revealed that the network contained no shared drives, although it had many actively connected employee computers.

Phish Using Smaller Fish

If the phish you caught with your phishing campaign is not high enough, you can use that phished user to capture other users. People tend to more readily trust the content of emails from someone they know, so here you are using that trust to send a malicious phishing email. Most people that identify phishing emails do not alert IT about them.

I found that Jing had sent a request for a transaction order execution to Ming. I found the original document and spiked it with an RAT. Then I attached the modified document and requested a simple confirmation from Ming that the transaction order in the attachment was executed. I scheduled to send the email in the morning around the time Jing usually walked past my network in the park. With no more actions on my agenda for the night, I deleted some logs and cleaned the history before logging off and heading to bed.

The next evening, I got confirmation that Ming had opened the email, so I logged into her computer. I also logged into Jing's computer and saw that Ming had replied to the email but that Jing had simply discarded it—at least digitally speaking. He could have gone and reported the email to the IT department in person, but I was doubtful about that, as in that case, it would have triggered an investigation and I would not have had access to the computer anymore. After I deleted the discarded email and cleared the logs and history, I logged off from Jing's computer. Ming's computer was in a different subdomain with a different Domain Name Server. I deployed the crawler bot to explore the network. This time, it did identify a couple of servers listening on various ports, so the mapping of possible targets started again. As the crawler bot began working again, I cleaned some logs and logged off. I cycled to my day job. After I came home from work, I prepared for a long night again. I had cooked risotto for dinner and put some Grana Padano on top of it. The food tasted great, and without electronic distractions, I enjoyed every bite. As I was eating dinner, I thought of the task at hand. Most likely, I had another evening and night of hacking the foreign network and discovering flaws in the whole system. I put the dishes in the dishwasher, took the chocolates out of the fridge, and prepared them next to the computer before giving a first glance at the crawler report. This way, I was eating in peace and was completely calm as I sat behind the computer.

The crawler's report identified only one server on the network. This indicated that the whole system was designed so that the cashier terminals were only connected to the banking database and banking software. There were no other targets to exploit except for the banking server. The intelligent design meant I only had this one target to exploit. But looking at the programs and versions that were installed, I noticed that besides banking software, an older version of the Tectia SSH server was installed. More explicitly, it was version 6.3.2, which had a nasty vulnerability, CVE-2012-5975, which enables attackers to bypass authentication.

Exploiting Vulnerability

Now that I knew how to log in to the server, I crafted the special session, which gained me root access to the server. I was able to install programs, cache messages, change programs, modify existing programs, and even add users. Now that I was on a server, I needed to somehow bypass the banking software and its connection to the inter-banking network. I had two options: either fake incoming transactions, which would get cashiers in trouble, or fake outgoing transactions to the inter-banking network. There was, of course, a third option, which involved trying to hack into the banking software and its database, but that would require at least some knowledge of the software and some exploration that I should not be doing on the live instance to avoid detection. I had installed a monitoring tool that would parse incoming and outgoing messages and try to extract some useful information like transaction IDs, values, bank accounts, and maybe even some authentication. Since both these connections were encrypted, I used the OpenSSH Heartbleed bug to extract useful data out of the data stream. All this was possible because my monitoring software acted as a middleman between the network interface and the banking software. Because I did this at night, when there were basically no transactions, I avoided detection from users or even the loss of some transactions. Now everything was set up, and to maintain permanent access to the server, I created a new ssh user in case they decided to update the ssh server in the next few days. Then I deleted all the logs of my activity and logged out.

After I logged out, I felt thrilled, but I was still quite a ways away from the successful money transfer. I needed more data. The strong IT infrastructure made this a lot more challenging, but poor IT management, which included not updating the kernel and software, made it possible again. I went to bed for few hours, but I needed at least one day of data monitoring to see if I could fake the transactions and start to automate that part of the process.

After I woke up in the morning to get ready for my day job, I felt sluggish, but this was not a time to get soft and cranky. I again biked to work to get my blood flowing, and after a shower in the office, I was fresh as a daisy until lunch. We had fries for lunch, which were so fatty that I got a bit drowsy in the afternoon. Luckily, riding my bicycle home woke me up, and as I got home, I just took Corn Flakes and a rice drink to get me refreshed and ready for another long evening. Another stack of chocolates next to my computer fueled my brain during this next exploration. I dug through the mountain of logs obtained by the monitoring tool. The sheer amount of data wrecked my brain as I tried to spot the sequences and then decode various parts of the messages. I needed to provide existing examples for my scripts to parse the rest of the data. I have yet to find a decent tool that will tell you if a message contains an eight-byte sequence number, a four-byte time stamp, a twelve-byte transaction id, etc. However, sometimes this is much easier. Most of my job was already complete before I even ate my first chocolate, as the software server was using the SOAP interface toward the inter-banking server. SOAP is an XML-based protocol that leaves everything from authentication to authorization entirely up to the software. And it is a lot easier to decode than just a binary blob. After looking at a couple of transaction requests and responses, I decided to write a script that mimicked the whole flow. I included a random execution pattern in the script, and because the script intercepted the communication with banking software as well as inter-banking server responses, the transactions were never listed in the banking software. The script ensured that the banking software was unaware of the transaction requests made on its behalf, and that the responses would be confirmed as if they had originated from the banking software. The script also cleared my tracks on the server and any logs, so I spent an evening on that and then prepared everything for the next Hong Kong working day, which was by then around six hours away. As everything was prepared, I set my alarm clock and quickly went to bed.

Cashing Out

My alarm woke me up early the next morning, my local time, but before the official States Bank opened at 9:00 a.m. Hong Kong time. I had enough time, so I went for a run. There were clouds outside, so it wasn't really too welcoming for a run, but when I started to move, my blood flow also increased. I felt tired and sleepy. As I ran past the residential area, I turned toward the forest paths. In my mind, I planned a short route because I did not have much time. I also went a bit slower so I could think about something else besides just moving my legs and breathing. In my mind, I went through all of the details again, although everything was prepared for cashing out. I doubted that they had detected my scripts or my logins, but this was still a real possibility that could end my operation before it even began. As I neared my house again, I was anxious to earn more money. I was already a millionaire, and I really did not need more money, but I wanted to maximize the profits of deploying the RaspberryPi mesh and getting this in motion. I also knew that once they spotted the first attack, they would probably revise how inter-banking transactions were made and tighten the security even more. This is how it always happens, and it raises the bar for the next guy as both sides compete against each other.

Prepare for the Money

After a shower and a breakfast of bread with chocolate spread, I was ready to start my day. The Hong Kong banks were already well into their opening hours, so as I logged into the hacked server, it meant I was going up against a fully prepared security team. If someone was watching the logged-in usernames or monitoring the network stream, they might detect me. Although the script was relatively small, it could still be flagged by some other monitoring tools. Anyway, my monitoring tools script had been executing for a full day already, and nobody had noticed it. I was doubtful that even processes on the server were actively monitored or equipped with alerts. That is why, in this particular case, I did not even need to mask my operation; it was all done independently from the banking software already.

As everything was ready, I simply executed the script and checked the SOAP message exchanges. The first 100 million US dollar purchases of gold, Monero cryptocurrency, and palladium went through without a hitch. So I scheduled a second and third batch to be spread out over the next four hours while I was working my day job. There was ample disk space to save my logs, so before leaving the script running, I cleared them to avoid any nasty surprises. I would not be able to monitor progress over the next thirty minutes as I needed to arrive at my office, so I didn't want any interactions or transactions then. After that, the transactions should be spread randomly throughout the rest of the day, which would again steal 400 million US dollars. As I drove to work, all I could think of was that they might detect the latest activity and set a trap for the next time I would login. I did not have to login until the evening as I was quite sure that the script had worked, but as I arrived at the office, I felt butterflies in my stomach. I logged on to the home VPN to hide any additional activity from the office, and I logged through the VPN to the banking server just in time for the transactions to start. I was basically not doing my day job as I watched the transactions complete. Luckily, we were not near any deadlines at work, so I could afford to slack off for a day, knowing I would replace it with work in the next few days and on the weekends. The transactions went smoothly again, so I left the server for a few hours before checking again. That's how my whole day went by. I could hardly think about anything else besides all the assets I was buying as order confirmations soon started pouring into my inbox. All the tracking information of everything that had been shipped started to come in as well. Before the end of the day in Hong Kong, I made sure I was back at my house. The final sum exchange of the transactions per day between the inter-banking server and banking software was the most crucial part of the covering operation. Without that, alerts would go off everywhere and I would most likely get detected. I did not move my eyes from the computer as the banking operational hours were completed at 5:00 p.m. on that day and the final summary exchange was done. The 400 million dollars I stole got officially confirmed by banking software, which actually thought it was confirming a number that was 400 million dollars lower than it actually was. It was almost a perfect crime. I started with deleting the initial RAT, the cashier RAT, and some other things on the banking software server. I made sure I deleted all the logs of my presence and all the activity, and then I also automated that action so that after the software was back up and running, the cleanup would be performed as well. That included erasing restart information from the banking software logs. Then I logged off. I set my alarm to just a bit after midnight Hong Kong time and went to prepare dinner. I was full of chocolate, so I wasn't that hungry, but I hadn't eaten anything warm the whole day. So I prepared a chop suey in a wok along with noodles and ate it on my dinner table away from the computer. I was already hearing alerts. The new confirmations of my purchases and tracking information were coming in, so it was not a quiet meal. As I finished eating and put everything into the dishwasher, I went to my computer and started checking all the cryptocurrency purchases and transferring them to my private wallets. To avoid any connection with the previous heist, I also used new wallets just as a precaution.

Covering the Tracks

As the alarm went off, reminding me that I still needed to perform my last cleanup, it was quite hard to focus. I logged back into the States Bank network and checked again for any additional activity while I was gone. I noticed none. Based on information from the logs, I knew that the network was quite dead after 11:00 p.m. Hong Kong time and that no new activity was detected at that moment as well. So I deleted the script and restarted the software. Now the banking software was again listening directly to the port, without my script in the middle. The restart took a few minutes, and I waited for the banking software to completely load. Then I cleaned the logs. As one example, all logs are usually time-stamped. This helps with debugging, but it also helps hackers who know precisely which parts of the logs need to be removed to cover up for the reboot. After that, I logged out from the user back to the root user, deleted the created user, cleaned up the history and logins, and then logged out of the server.

Collecting the Assets

The plan to obtain gold and palladium in my possession was not complicated. I had prepared addresses in Panama and the Cayman Islands for this reason, but I also added the addresses of some of the abandoned houses where mailmen dropped the packages. Tracking a thousand packages was an experience only logistic managers at big companies have, but none of them had experience with the value of these shipments. This was one of the points of the plan where everything could go wrong. Still, it was vital to be as fast as possible. By then, just a few days after the attack, I was in possession of 550 million US dollars in gold and palladium. The warehouses I rented would contain something like 7,436 boxes of around 100 kg palladium or gold coins. That was a massive amount of decently heavy boxes, but luckily for me, they did not all arrive at the same time. The first weekend, not even half the boxes came, and to reduce the risk, I had to disperse them enough in case one got compromised or looted. No vault could store them, and I definitely did not want to rent one in the system I had just compromised.

It was the first weekend after the hack, and while many of the shipments had already arrived at the warehouses, I decided to pick whatever one arrived early and take care of everything else later. I knew the authorities would be most vigilant with people who traveled to the shipment destinations on dates close to the heist, so I had to be extra careful. I returned back to my blonde hair and shortly trimmed beard look, which had led to some interesting encounters the last time around. I was certain now that Alice and Elise and even Pam were not undercover agents or detectives, so before the weekend, I finally opened the email address I shared with them for the first time. I had gotten mail from both Alice and Elise. While Alice was still in Miami, I asked Elise where she was traveling this weekend. She had a long-distance flight from Panama City to Paris, which I could use on my return trip. Again, she would have an overnight stay in Panama City, so I needed to get a direct flight to the Cayman Islands first. The flight was either from London or Frankfurt airport. I was reluctant to go through UK airports, as the security there seemed a lot tighter, so I picked Frankfurt. However, that meant I had to drive at least some of the way, and it was a relatively long drive. But I decided quickly and reserved the flight and then separately booked a return flight from Tocumen Airport. It meant that I had a bit less time in the Cayman Islands to find and buy a suitable property and then stash part of the assets that were already in that warehouse while leaving the rest there for pickup later. The plan needed adjusting as initially, I wanted to transfer some of the assets from Panama City to the Cayman Islands. Still, it seemed more comfortable to just buy another place in Panama City where I could hide the assets that had already arrived.

Flight to the Cayman Islands

Mornings at airports are always very peaceful. The early morning transcontinental flights basically fly so early, most of the people are not even on their way to the airport. Frankfurt Airport's atmosphere is no different. Because of the early flight, I was driven to the airport's vicinity by car on Friday evening. I slept in a small village not far from the airport and ordered an early morning taxi to pick me up. As soon as I arrived in the room, I went to sleep. The excitement of being a millionaire started to settle in. I could have afforded a better hotel, but I did not want to spend the hard-earned money for some unnecessary luxury. As I woke in the middle of the night and got to the taxi, the streets were totally empty. The airport was not crowded either, so I could quickly get a boarding pass from the check-in machine. After that, I walked to security, where I casually put all my belongings into the box and just walked through the metal detector. There was also no queue for the police check, but as I was walking past other security points, the staff looked at my blond hair and beard a bit longer than I would have expected. As I stood near the gate, I noticed that it was full of couples and families going on vacation. I tried not to stand out from the crowd, so once we boarded the airplane, I just quickly sat down. I was soon joined by a family. During the flight, many kids were jumping around, so I could not watch a movie. It was quite different than previous weekends, as after takeoff, it was a nonstop party. The kids behaved well during the meals, so I enjoyed the company, and the time passed quickly. As I went to stretch my legs in the flight attendant section of the airplane, it was almost a relief to enjoy some silence. The meals tasted excellent again, and I tried to get some sleep, but I was only able to catch two quick naps. Nothing unusual was on that flight, although I was expecting some police in case my activity a few days ago had been discovered. I would not imagine the police using families with kids as undercover agents, so I was not suspicious. From time to time, I looked around the airplane to see if some of the passengers were paying extra attention to me, but I was soon calmed by the fact that everyone was minding their own business. When we landed in the Cayman Islands in the morning, I calmly walked through the terminal and past police and customs control at the airport.

Cayman Islands Gold and Palladium Pickup

The excitement started to grow as I was approaching the warehouse, which had received my assets. I had received the notifications of the shipment delivery of around 200 boxes already, and tracking indicated about 600 more would arrive that day. I went around the building to make sure there were no police and looked around before entering the building. The receptionist greeted me and then escorted me to the warehouse storage box. The 200 kg of gold and palladium is not that much in storage. I took this opportunity to take some of the palladium and gold coins from the warehouse. I put them in my bag and closed the door. On my way out, I greeted the receptionist with a huge smile. While I was already a cryptocurrency millionaire, with more than 200 million US dollars in cryptocurrencies, this was the first time I was also an ordinary millionaire. My path took me toward the bank in George Town, where I sold and deposited the gold and palladium coins into my Cayman Island company's bank account. From the bank, I walked to the real estate agency in the center, where I had a few appointments already set up to look at some real estate in town. After visiting the places, I just signed the contract for the one I liked the most. It was located very close to the beach and had a basement. Then I rented a minivan and moved all the received shipments from the storage room to the new estate. The time flew by, and soon it was time for the late afternoon flight to the Tocumen Airport in Panama City. I took a few gold coins in my backpack that mimicked my wallet's change. They were worth more than 1 million US Dollars. I anxiously went through the security check, but there weren't any problems, and soon, I flew from the Cayman Islands. I took a nap on the empty flight. When I woke up, I checked around the airplane again to see if I was being watched, but I did not notice anything suspicious.

Panama City Gold and Palladium Pickup

I landed at Tocumen Airport in the late evening. Fortunately, the customs check was not really interested in whether or not I had anything to declare, so I was out of the terminal fast. I waited for Elise at a hotel while surfing the internet for new real estate in Panama City. I just needed something small—nothing too flashy —that was located in a bit more remote part of town. I already had a couple of visits planned for the next morning, but I still found one more place just as Elise entered. I stood up and gave her a long hug, and she seemed equally happy. This time, of course, she asked me why I was there, and when I told her I would be on her flight back to Paris as well, she was delighted. She told me she could take a few days off in Paris, but I told her that it was not possible for me to take such a vacation now. I had to follow the plan to the last detail if I wanted to succeed in the end. I also told her I had a few meetings the next morning but that I would hopefully be back in the hotel for lunch. We spent an eventful evening, and early the next morning, I was already on my way to the warehouse to pick up some more gold, which I then deposited into my Panama company's account. I went and looked at some real estate in Panama City with the real estate agent. I soon found a perfect place next to the forest, which was included with the property. I signed the contract with the owner, transferred the money, and got the keys. Then I quickly rented a van and drove to the warehouse to pick up the bags that had already been delivered to the property. I hid most of the stuff in the apartment and then dug a hole, with the shovel I found in the basement on the property, under the biggest tree to hide the remainder. I marked the location with the GPS coordinates just in case. I was done just in time for lunch, so I went back to the hotel and took Elise out to eat. She knew a lot of good places, so I let her choose. I was constantly scanning the vicinity with my eyes, which Elise noticed and joked about. I could not tell her the details. However, I did ask her to carry two of my big golden and palladium coins to Paris. It was a minor ask for her since the coins were worth less than 10,000 euros, and I told her I had gotten paid for a job in coins to avoid the tax hit and that I would like to bring them to Europe. There is a 10,000-euro limit on money and assets; above that you are obligated to declare them to customs. That is why I wanted to split the coins between us. I did not mention that, in fact, I was carrying considerably more than that. You might know this, but gold coins in smaller formats look a lot like regular coins. Of course, they are usually protected, but for this trip, I would take them out of their casings and put them into the change purse in my bag. On the X-Ray machine, they would be visible as ordinary coins, and I have yet to find the customs officer who would check a small pocket change wallet. Also, you go through X-Ray on departure only, while usually, you can just walk past the customs at the EU airports. I spent the rest of the afternoon with Elise in Panama City before she departed for her flight. About an hour later, I also got into a taxi and was driven to the airport. I had twenty small golden coins nicely in my coin bag, and I replaced all fourteen coins in my wallet with golden coins. The overall worth was not that much, but it would still help me get through the week without additional complications.

Flight to Paris with a Bag of Gold

It was a very productive weekend, and now both my companies' accounts had more than 50 million US dollars in their accounts. While this is usually enough to buy any real estate, I had far more investments planned for the next year. I still wanted to keep my appearance for the year by living like a regular guy. Once at the airport, I again went to the check-in machine to get my boarding pass. The security line was long, so I patiently waited in the queue. Elise was already bored and on board the airplane, sending me emails. This was when she asked me for a WhatsApp account or something to have the instant messaging capability. I wanted to propose the Telegram app, but that would have taken as much time to set up as it would take to get to the plane, so I just explained it to her like that. After a couple more emails, I was already next to the security check. Writing with Elise totally took my edge off, so I was completely relaxed going through the X-Ray machine with my handbag full of gold coins. As my bag was selected for a manual personal check, my heart started to pump. Had Elise been caught, and had she told them that the gold she was carrying was actually mine? The security guard politely asked me if he could open the bag. If there was ever a time I really wanted to say NO, it was now. I mean, is it even worth it to say no? What would they do then, wait for a court order? I calmly replied that he could open the bag and have a look. As he was opening the bag, he went through its contents, such as my toothbrush and my file with contracts in it. He never touched the change wallet at the bottom of the bag—if he had, he would have noticed it was heavier than expected. Then he told me to have a nice flight. My heart was pounding like crazy as I put my stuff back and headed over to the police checkup. There was also a queue there, so I wrote to Elise. Of course, I did not mention the random check and just continued the conversation. At the police check, they only glanced at me and then waved me through. Boarding had already started, and while I was boarding the Airbus A380, the gate agent told me that Elise had upgraded me to Special Class for this flight and that I should go to seat 1X. It was a pleasant surprise as well because if someone had been waiting for me around my designated seat, they would have thought I had not boarded. As I boarded the airplane, I asked the first flight attendant where seat 1X was, and it put a huge smile on her face. She said, "Just go up the stairs through first class, and she is already waiting for you there." I guess it really pays off to know flight attendants, and as I was walking through first class, Elise was there. She knocked on the cockpit and introduced me to the pilot. The pilot was very friendly and offered me a jumper seat in the cockpit for the time being. As Elise was handling the first-class passengers, the pilot and her copilot were going through the preflight checklist. I was familiar with the A380 from the *FlightGear* flight simulator I had played in the past and recognized the controls. However, being in a cockpit full of people handling this airplane, transporting more than 500 people at once, was a truly amazing experience. As boarding was completed, Elise invited me to an empty seat in first class. She told me to sit there for takeoff and that she would take good care of me. The first class on an A380 is just amazing, yet small, but the business class upper deck has a lot of space. It is not like first-class passengers would even want to leave the seat, which has a lot of space, reclines into a full bed, and offers all the luxury you could imagine. As we took off, Elise did her first round through the passengers. She skipped me, or better, saved me for the last. As she got me an orange juice, she told me to come to stretch my legs in the front. Tempting as it was to just jump after her, walking behind a flight attendant does raise some eyes. I waited a couple of seconds before I went to stretch my legs. She said we could talk easily at the front, as she should not be seen favoring one of the passengers. While we were talking, we paused for a bit so that she could respond to passengers' requests, but otherwise, we had time to talk. I was just sipping my orange juice as the time flew by, and I got to know her better and better. As we talked, I avoided sharing too much of my personal information just in case she would ever be questioned by the police. I shared with her the life story I'd developed for my fictional identity, so she did not have any information connecting to my real life. It enabled me to still play the stolen identity card in the future. Meals in first class are indeed a lot better and also have more variation. I enjoyed the whole flight, and the time passed by really quickly. Soon we were landing in Paris. After we landed, reality kicked back in. I was carrying more gold than I was allowed. Explaining the origin of the coins and also my story of a stolen identity might get me in trouble in this case. After all, I could not tell stuff from my real identity, and the lies, if checked, could get me in trouble with the police. And I assumed that they would check everything in such a case. As I was leaving the plane, I was thinking of telling Elise that in case something happened, she could keep the coins. I focused on the positive and said nothing. I walked from the plane to the airport exit in a crowd. It was a long walk, and because everybody seemed to be walking fast, it was a nice reminder to try to not fall behind. I did not want to be singled out from the crowd. As I approached the customs check, I automatically went to the "Nothing to Declare" lane. As I was walking by, none of the officers there reacted. I kept walking toward the parking lot where I waited for Elise. I had managed to get a bag of gold into Europe. As Elise arrived, we took a taxi and spent the whole evening in Paris. In the early morning, a friend came and picked me up. When we arrived at my house, I got on my bike and rode it to the office as usual. Nobody there suspected I had been halfway around the globe over the weekend, and everything continued as usual.

Cleanup of the Physical Devices

A few weeks after the hack, as all the devices were already completely wiped, their batteries also died. I was surprised that there was no news about the cyberattack in the various security-related media I followed. I was not naive; they should have uncovered it for sure, and most likely, the full investigation was underway. Since the devices reported no alerts, I had a high level of confidence that they hadn't been breached or even discovered.

Flying to Hong Kong

A couple of weeks after the hack, I reserved a weekend flight from the Amsterdam International Airport to Singapore Changi Airport. I booked another flight five hours after arriving from Singapore to Hong Kong, where I also reserved a hotel for the first night. My day started early as I arrived in my office before everyone else. Not long after lunch, I drove home to color my beard and hair with the foxy orange color again and then drove to the Amsterdam Airport's vicinity to catch an evening flight. I parked in a nearby village and went quickly on the first bus that went by. I arrived at the airport soon enough to calmly print my boarding pass at a check-in machine. I headed through security and ended in a long queue. I still had ample time, so I was not worried, but this gave me time to look around. Nobody was looking directly at me, and the security check went normally. The police point was also just basically a walk-through, and I was already walking toward the gates for boarding. I was again ahead of schedule, and that meant I had to find a toilet to hide for the next thirty minutes until boarding was well underway. As I came out from the toilet, the boarding was almost complete. I showed my boarding pass and walked down the hallway toward the airplane. I sat between an older, casually dressed guy and a young student. We greeted each other and that was about it for the whole flight. Even before takeoff, I was already watching movies to ease my mind. I was tired after a long day, so I fell asleep quickly. I slept through the first meal and woke up just in time for the second one. The meal was barely enough, as I was hungry. I restarted the movie, during which I fell asleep, and it ended just as we landed. At the Singapore Airport, I walked for fifteen minutes toward the exit. As I exited the airport, I just took a taxi that would take me one street away from the warehouse. I went toward the storage facility and walked around it a couple of times to ensure there were no people watching from cars or nearby buildings. As I entered the storage box, it was literally full of shipments. I took enough golden coins to make them look like my change and took an additional two one-ounce pieces so I could have cash for the trip. As I walked back toward the bus stop, I noticed a few guys looking at me from afar. I decided to quickly signal a taxi that was driving nearby to avoid any unpleasant confrontation. They looked more like street thugs than undercover police. As I approached the airport, I quickly went through security. I at least wanted to be in an international space before getting something to eat. The security check took no notice of my cargo, and the police check went swiftly as well. I was hungry, so I picked the Burger King for a quick bite just in case the boarding had already started. As boarding began, I was already at the gate, so I sat in the airplane for some time, watching the people get seated. Nobody was traveling light or focusing on me, which made me a bit more comfortable after the street encounter. The first meal on the flight to Hong Kong was chicken with noodles and a brownie for dessert; that was a fun combination, as I doubt the Chinese knew brownies. I again watched movies, as I was quite refreshed after my sleep on the previous flight. Upon landing at the Hong Kong airport, I went straight to the hotel.

Dispose of All Physical Evidence

It was a late night, but I had reserved a hotel room and it was waiting for me. I only took the key and left the hotel again. I went into a nearby gold shop to exchange the golden coin for Hong Kong dollars. I had a map printed out of the device's location, a photo of the device, and the price next to it. I also had another printed map of where I would leave the money. I had to hide it first. I made sure to wear thin gloves, and I also put on a baseball cap just in case. First, I set the envelopes with money in an alley, then I walked around the park to find some homeless people. I thought finding people on the street would be easier, but it was not. I found a few of them under the nearby motorway bridge and handed out three papers. As they each walked to the devices, I observed them from afar to see if there would be any movement by the police. Presence in a physical location to remove evidence is proof of involvement that not even the best lawyer can dispute. If you knew where the devices were hidden, then you were the one placing them there in the first place. The homeless people I had hired found all three devices and picked them up. Each carried them to their own dumpster before returning to me. I gave them an equivalent of 300 US dollars in an envelope, and they thanked me very politely. I gave them another set of maps to dispose of the GPRS hubs that were behind the climber plants and in the pots. Each of them also got a map of the payout money location. It gave me enough time to move aside and then watch from afar while not having contact with them anymore in case they were being observed in more detail now. Each of them was happy with the money they got for the previous task, so they played it fair for this one as well. They all found the devices and threw them into big dumpsters on the street before walking toward the money. I did not wait to see if they actually found the money, and I went toward the hotel, using an extremely circuitous route. When I arrived at the hotel, it was early morning, and I just wanted to rest for a few hours.

Flying Back Home

Hong Kong Airport is vast, so you need to take ample time to get to the gates. As I woke up in the late morning, I decided to take the fast train from the city to the airport. I probably did not look rested, but I would have enough time to sleep on the plane home. The train and public places also allowed me to observe more closely if I was being followed. Because it was crowded, I could also easily disappear into the crowd in case there was strange activity. I wanted to be out of Hong Kong soon, as this was the place where I had committed my illegal activities. On the train, I did not spot anyone who seemed too interested in my movements or seemed to be following me. It felt the same at the airport. I went through security without a problem, even though there was literally gold in my bag. At the police check, I also was basically just glanced over, and suddenly I felt a big relief. If I was a suspect, they would not let me go. I exchanged my remaining HK dollars for euros at a terrible exchange rate and threw the receipt away. Nothing in my possession should connect me to Hong Kong, so it was all about not being sentimental and keeping souvenirs. Hong Kong Airport has a train to the gates, but I was no longer constantly looking over my shoulder. I was just blending in with the crowd, and when I arrived at the gate, boarding had already started. I again got on the plane early and observed the people boarding. This time, two young Asians sat near the window beside me, and I could not decipher anything they were saying. We were already on the runway when one of them seemed to get bored and started asking me questions about where I was going and where I was from. I was replying politely when the pilot told us that the plane was indicating some problem and that we needed to taxi back to the gate to check it out. My stress level rose, but I was still keeping a calm and composed look. The various scenarios went through my mind, from how I could be uncovered to how I could escape if I needed to. After we parked, the engineer came on board, and the flight attendants gave us some complimentary drinks and chocolates. At that moment, I was no longer worried; I doubted the police would first send an engineer before rushing in to arrest me. After the engineer left, we were on our way again. The first meal came right after takeoff, and I was so hungry from the stress that it tasted great. I was tired from the adrenaline and soon fell fast asleep.

Elise dropped by my seat and greeted me. That was a strange surprise as I thought she more regularly flew the Atlantic routes rather than the Asian ones. She was surprised by my foxy orange style and said she wasn't sure that it was me. At first, I thought this was too big of a coincidence, but because my cover was already blown, I told her all about my recent flying adventures. Her business management studies could also help me lead my companies. So we went to the back of the plane to chat a bit. I told her I would explain it all when we got to her hotel room, and her naughty look told me that she didn't even care about the explanation. As we landed and went through the terminal, I was totally carefree, so I just waited for her outside of the terminal so we could go to the hotel together. In the hotel room, I opened my backpack to show her the golden coins. She was surprised that I got paid in gold and once again asked me what I did for a living. I told her that she already knew the truth about my day job but that I recently managed to transfer some funds from some banks to buy gold and other assets. She was almost starting to strip and then stopped. She looked at me and said, "Oh, I thought you were a contract hitman or something. Do you think they found out about you?"

"I made it home from the city where I committed the crime. I doubt that they have spotted anything. Also, my systems alerts were not triggered, so they are either really good, or I was not detected," I replied.

She did not want to know the details, so we just continued the wild night. When morning came, she had to go to work. I knew that it would take her a couple of weeks to come back to my part of the world, and I was sorry to see her go. After she left, I made a plan to propose to her on the island where I would buy some property to live. I knew she liked tropical islands from her blog and that she likes to be spoiled, so I reserved an expensive resort to which I invited her for vacation. The Cook Islands seemed like a perfect place to live with her as well, so that's where I proposed, and she delightfully accepted. With the money, we built ourselves a self-sufficient villa with a lot of land around it to ensure our privacy. Soon she was pregnant, and after two kids, we lived a happy life. One day, we got into an argument because I did not want to go on a ski vacation in China because Hong Kong is part of China, and I assumed it was too risky. She insisted, and after a few days just told me, "I cannot live like this. I am going to leave you and take the kids with me."

"I have the right to see my kids," I replied.

"If you demand them legally, I will inform the authorities about your past actions and present them all the proof they need," she threatened me.

I did not think she would do it, so I kept insisting, and one early morning, the special police forces rushed into my house, kicking the door down and shouting.

That's when I woke up to the announcement: "We are about to land in Amsterdam Schiphol Airport, please go to your seat and fasten your seat belts." To my relief, it had all been a dream. After landing, I went through the terminal and customs without a problem and took a bus from the Amsterdam Airport to the nearby village where I burned the boarding pass. I got in my car and drove home.

So at this point, my plan was basically complete, and all the physical evidence was disposed of. Most of the gold was still in the warehouses, far from a secure or safe location, but before I had executed the plan, I did not have enough money to buy properties around the world where I could hide gold and palladium. Now I had enough of it in both companies' accounts to actually start looking for properties where I could spend the rest of my life. I remained in Europe for the time being, but it would be great to have a holiday location where I could still perform my job without being under the constant supervision and surveillance of modern technology. Likewise, arrest warrants are only valid in certain countries, so finding one without an extradition treaty would also increase my chances of enjoying my wealth.

A Year after the Hack

I was well aware of my surroundings the whole time after the hack. I spent time at my day job in the office and tried to find ways to spend the money without getting noticed. The cryptocurrencies grew during that time, as did the value of gold and palladium, which meant that without doing anything, my wealth was growing.

I requested a new passport, claiming I had misplaced my old one after traveling less frequently. After all, I did not want to be seen flying to the same destinations, and since both Alice and Elise were based in Miami, I had little hope of ever meeting either of them ever again. That was for the best, as both of them were the only thing connecting me to either of those trips. I can say life tends to go on when we just leave some people behind, and today all that remains is a nice memory. One year after the hack, I also minimized any of my security-associated activities, like visiting training sites for hacking or even vulnerability exposure events and bounty programs. There was also no real need to take any risks. After all, with the money I had obtained and secured, I would be able to live luxuriously for the rest of my life. And if I had kids, they also would be able to get a pretty decent start.

Buying the Island

The best way to hide a large amount of money is to use a shell company to buy a property and then store your boxes there. I was looking for a cheap island in the middle of the Pacific Ocean. Most islands there are uninhabited because they do not have drinking water. Transporting anything to a remote island can be challenging, so the island needs to be big enough to land a decent plane. I glanced at the Marshall Islands, but the US military had conducted nuclear tests there (and who knows what else), so I was not really interested in moving there. Then the Cook Islands became an option, but there were too many tourists. I did have a trip planned there for vacation, of course. South of those islands, and a bit more to the east, you find the tiny island countries of Fiji, Tonga, and the British Virgin Islands. While the first two were an option, the British Virgin Islands were not. For one thing, it was a closed community. The British jurisdiction system was in place there as well. I also took a long look at Niue Island. It is part of New Zealand, although it is quite far away and has a milder climate, meaningless poisonous animals, and hot summers. Property there is usually not available often. However, I was lucky. The year after the heist, many properties became available that both my Cayman Island and Panama companies were able to buy. On the new properties, I made plans to install solar panels and build a rain collection plant to collect drinking water and wind turbines to provide electricity. I also bought shares in a certain fast-growing satellite broadband internet company that had recently started launching satellites into orbit. Boats delivered the food, or I could catch fish in the lagoon. To get a legal income and later a pension plan, the shell company employed me to perform various fictional tasks, which brought in a nice salary every month.

Detection and Public Disclosure Dilemma

For an entire year, there was no disclosure of the bank robbery mentioned anywhere. Usually, when a security team detects an intrusion, they first close the network even more tightly and then launch an investigation. If they are smart, they also invite some external security experts for help, and usually, it is just a matter of time before they connect the dots in terms of how the intrusion happened. The question after all that is: Do you publicly disclose and confirm the breach or not? If you confirm a security breach, then you usually suffer commercial consequences along with the loss of trust of your customers and, most likely, some fines from a regulatory institution or privacy agency according to the GDPR for not protecting privacy. If an organization hides everything, they perform internal cleanup and try to punish the hackers covertly. Financial institutions are under quite tight regulatory regulations, so I was expecting a notification of the police and then at least some news, but none of that was published within that first year. I started wondering if they even detected the missing money, but I was sure that in the end of the year balance, they would detect it, if not sooner. I vividly imagined someone having to tell the CEO that there was a 450 million US dollar difference between the incoming and outgoing transactions in the inter-bank system, which did not match the local bank database. Also, since it was an inter-banking system, multiple banks needed to check their budgets and balances to confirm that this was indeed originating from the bank I hacked. So I imagine it was not a really short and optimized process to begin with. And because we are talking about the inter-banking network, a public disclosure that it was vulnerable and that money had been stolen from it would have a worldwide impact on all the banks and how they approached this. It would also mean that there was no easy fix and that before adequate protection could be provided, other hackers would have the opportunity to exploit the system as well. As more time passed from the hack, there was less and less of a chance that they would uncover me or even find some physical evidence to trace the hack's real origin. The RaspberryPi network, along with the SIM cards and all the hardware were trashed in the container park. IP traces and activity logs are also slowly rotated and deleted over time, and that severely impacts the efficiency of the investigation. Based on that, at the end of the year, I was pretty confident that they would not be able to trace me or connect me to any of the crimes.

Disclaimer

The events portrayed in this book are all fictional. While some ideas involved in the illegal setup could be used in practice, the author takes no responsibility for such actions, nor does he condone them. Most of the book describes one or another illegal activity, which includes serious consequences, including jail time or even the death sentence in some countries and some organizations. The purpose of this book was not to promote such activity but to make people aware of the current capabilities of even hobby projects, where simple board computers and tools that are available to the public can greatly impact information security everywhere.

The content is written in the first person, from the eyes of the criminal, to make it more personal and plausible, but in reality, Joncy Ber is a fictional person, and any similarity to existing events or persons is purely accidental.

About the Author

Crt Mori is an embedded software engineer who is passionate about spy stories and detective thrillers. He is new at writing his own stories as he usually writes technical documents.

Born in Ljubljana, Slovenia, he now lives and works in Belgium, where he has settled with his family. He has a lot of hobby projects, mostly with embedded devices that make everyday chores and repeatable tasks easier. As those projects are mostly exposed to internet, he is also a computer security enthusiast.

He writes a personal blog and technical tutorials on https://crt.the-mori.com.